PRAISE FOR *TRAGIC MAGIC*

"A prescient ancestor to today's insurgent, boundary-breaching African American fiction... deserves rediscovery by a new generation of readers curious about where an earlier generation of Black protest came from and how they came through its challenges." —*Kirkus*

"Personal courage, the nature of manhood (and womanhood), the ties of the past and the freedom held out by the future, all emerge as moving motifs... This jaunty prose version of the urban blues deserves an attentive audience." —*The New York Times*

"*Tragic Magic* is a signifyin dazzler in which Black vernacular does what it does: be dance, battle, and thesis. This sentence-level prestidigitation mirrors the narrative's tricky syncopation of tension and release, radical past and post-Civil Rights present, acid humor and the woe behind a wolf ticket's bluster. First published in 1978, Wesley Brown's remarkable and cinematic satire is still on-time, which is perhaps nearly as tragic as it's surely magical."
—Douglas Kearney, author of *Starts Spinning*

"*Tragic Magic* is a tremendous affirmation... One hell of a writer."
—James Baldwin

"Wonderfully wry."
—Donald Barthelme

"A clearly talented new writer."
—*Publishers Weekly*

"An important discovery."
—Ishmael Reed

"A literary gem."
—Mat Johnson

TRAGIC MAGIC

McSWEENEY'S

SAN FRANCISCO

We're grateful to Kevin Moffett who first brought this book to our attention, and to Concord Free Press and its co-founder and editor-in-chief Stona Fitch, whose yearslong support of Mr. Brown's work helped bring this edition to fruition.

Cover illustration by Sunra Thompson

ISBN 978-1-944211-98-1

10   9   8   7   6   5   4   3   2   1

www.mcsweeneys.net

Printed in Canada

TRAGIC MAGIC

A NOVEL

WESLEY BROWN

PART OF THE *OF THE DIASPORA* SERIES
edited by ERICA VITAL-LAZARE

McSWEENEY'S
SAN FRANCISCO

For my mother and father
and
Ted Solotaroff

———

"...A THING NEVER MEANT a thing until it moved." Melvin
Ellington, the protagonist of Wesley Brown's 1978 novel *Tragic
Magic* arrives at this realization, ironically, during one of the
few moments in the novel when he's at rest, finally lying at his
belle Alice's side. It's a posture we aren't used to seeing him in.
Magic covers a single day in Melvin's life as he makes his way
to New York City from Pennsylvania, where he served time for
refusing to be drafted into the Vietnam War. Thrown off his
path as a college student and finding himself marooned in a kind
of emotional dead zone—the result of steeling his heart against
the depravities of prison life—he walks his old neighborhood
haunts like a latter-day Leopold Bloom, if Bloom's step and
thought were infused with the spirit of jazz.

When the novel opens, Melvin's in transit. Riding a New
York City subway with a past date named Tonya, he sees a
man come onto her. The moment makes him insecure; should
he have stood up to the man on Tonya's behalf? Fought him?
"I guess I should have done something," he wonders aloud, like
he's playing for forgiveness. It's not forthcoming, because Tonya

isn't offended by his inaction in the least. "What could you have done?" she retorts. She rejects the notion that Melvin's gender makes it his duty to defend her honor—she's perfectly well off defending it herself, as she reminds him. "You know, I almost kicked that dude in his family jewels. I caught myself just in time. I guess that wouldn't have made you look too good if I had." Melvin finds himself anxious over Tonya's implication: that she doesn't need him around at all. At least, not in the tired, predictable ways he wants her to need him.

Tragic Magic is about tragedy, alright—the kinds of tragedies men bring upon themselves by allowing their inner lives to be ensnared in the trap we've come to call toxic masculinity; and the death of mind, spirit, and body that ensues when men willingly lower themselves into the coffin of gender expectations, how that death pervades everything from friendships to political activism. The scene is the first of many haunted by the specter of this death. When Melvin finds himself in a Pennsylvania prison preparing to serve a three-year bid for dodging the Vietnam War draft, he meets Chilly, an old hand of incarcerated life who warns him that not appearing like a certain kind of man can mean death. Or, worse, the ultimate violation of normative masculinity—sex between men. To that end, Chilly gives Melvin a set of directives: "Watch yourself when you take a shower. Don't walk around half nude. And for your own protection, make sure you stay on a top bunk. The main thing is to be a man."

But, as Brown suggests, being a man is dangerous business. When Melvin finds himself staring at another man's body in the prison shower, he indulges in gorgeous description, some of the novel's most beautiful writing. "The slouch in his shoulders is an indication that very little has impressed him enough to make him straighten up. His face interests me most of all," he rhapsodizes. "His hair, sideburns, and mustache have been trimmed as evenly as a well-kept lawn. And he is the color of a skillet broken in by cooking." He catches himself, though, remembering where he is. "I've got to be more careful... At any moment someone may decide you will make a good piece of merchandise."

Wesley Brown's genius in this novel is to set us down in the midst of men whose interior lives, whose senses of what it is possible for them to be in this world, have been so constrained by masculinity that they cannot even begin to think of other possibilities. He holds us so close to this world that it can seem as if there is no escaping it. Melvin, whose peers nickname him Mouth because of his overenthusiastic method of smooching women, is in many ways the perfect vehicle for this portrayal: his voice brings us into a too-intimate, almost claustrophobic relationship with the anxious world of masculinity, a community of men who feel a constant need to prove their male bona fides. It is a world of rampant homophobia, misogyny, body shaming, and generalized fear of what it would mean to let one's guard down and participate in an actually intimate relationship—not just with women, but with anybody at all. Melvin, who seems most motivated by an adolescent lust, is not exempt from this fraternity. As a result, neither is the reader.

We must be careful to read this novel not as an endorsement of heteronormativity, but an attempt to honestly reckon with the toll it takes on the novel's male characters, the way it leaves them emotionally deformed.

Among these men, Melvin's childhood friend Otis is perhaps the most deformed. A veteran of the Vietnam War who, unlike Melvin, was driven to fight by his obsession with that paragon of American machismo, John Wayne, Otis is a young buck whose chief concerns are bedding women and demonstrating his physical prowess against other men. Quick to anger and possessed of a pride that goes only about half an inch deep, he is the Kurtz to Melvin's Marlow. Racked by loneliness and more than a little guilt, Melvin seeks his friend out upon hearing that he's lost a hand as a result of the war. What he finds is less a person than an open wound, a man whose notion of his identity has been fundamentally challenged by his participation in a failed war, and a more personal failure to live up to an impossible standard. Once certain that fighting would make him every bit as heroic as Wayne, Otis—now a radio engineer rather than a warrior—is straining at society's leash, leaping at every chance he gets to prove his belonging to the lethal fraternity of American cowboys.

If Melvin is different from men like Otis, it is by virtue of his fundamentally curious nature. A skeptic whose posture towards life is characterized by a fundamental uncertainty, and an outsider who cannot quite fit himself into the cohort of horny alpha males who dominate his world, Melvin is attuned to a certain dissonance in the given world, the possibility that the world can be otherwise than it is. He is not a critic of this world but a questioner, a rebel without commitment to anything in particular, save what seems to be a pathological inability to accept things as they've been given to him—or to tell a story that doesn't zig and zag in an ecstatic direc-tionless-ness. Listening to Melvin think is like listening to Charlie Parker improvise a solo by following an idea or concept wherever it will take him, without any concern for whether or not it lines up with what came before, or what people will think of it.

And, just like "Bird's playing started everyone in the joint to jumping giddy and yapping in a strange tongue that empha-sized the buzzing sound of the letter Z," Melvin's improvisatory, itinerant thought process is an intimation of a new and different language of gender and masculinity. He sees and hears what his brethren cannot—or are unwilling to—see and hear. Back in the prison shower, for example, he perceives that the prison doesn't really mandate one strict definition of masculinity. Far from it: it's a space where men routinely break their own rules about what it means to "be a man." Melvin realizes that even as his fellow prisoners enforce certain gender norms, they themselves are "indulging in a favorite shower-room pastime: comparing the size of each other's Swanson Johnson." There's some kind of improvisation happening here, a possible riff on staid, boring heteronormativity, maybe a new language. The inmates engage in a comparison of virility, a test of manhood that will be "determined by the one who can get his rizz-od as hizz-ard as a rizz-ock at a mizz-oments nizz-otice."

The spirit of Bird lingers over the proceedings, shepherding us towards something other than a dangerous and tragic notion of the masculine. This is the gift that Wesley Brown has given us: a new way to speak, a language that we have to excavate and rescue from the murky depths of gender expectation. This novel is an unruly and difficult story of how gender works in the world, and how we might find our ways to new modes of being. This is a novel that denounces reification and casts off stasis in favor of itinerant movement, in the hopes that we might come to find the meaning of our lives by playing our own solos, by riffing on the given world in search of other possibilities.

—ISMAIL MUHAMMAD

INTRODUCTION

THE CONSUMMATE SHORT-STORY WRITER Grace Paley once said that, more often than not, the only thing coming with publication is silence. She, no doubt, meant that even glowing reviews from mainstream arbiters of culture, such as the *New York Times*, did not guarantee a substantial number of readers who would buy the book. This was my experience when my first novel, *Tragic Magic*, was published by Random House in the fall of 1978 and received enthusiastic reviews, particularly in the Sunday *New York Times Book Review*, but did not translate into sales. However, I felt enormously fortunate to have been one of the numerous African American writers that Toni Morrison guided to publication in the 1970s, during her many years as a senior editor at Random House.

I've thought a great deal about Paley's comment regarding the deafening "silence" that often greets publication since McSweeney's contacted me regarding their desire to republish my first novel. But what I'd like to revisit is not the silence in the aftermath of publication, but the presence of sounds, spoken and instrumental, that informed and continue to animate my experience of writing fiction.

The sounds of my mother and father's voices, the conversations overheard among aunts and uncles, the gossip between my sister and her girlfriends, and the lively barbershop talk are imprinted on nearly every page of *Tragic Magic*. There was also rhythm and blues and jazz that was baked into my nervous system.

I was reminded of this when rereading the opening of *Tragic Magic*: "A Few Words Before the Get Go." The narrator identifies with the improvisational approach of jazz musicians and decides to tell his story by "...play(ing) against the melody, behind and ahead of the beat, to bend, diminish, and flatten notes, and slip in and out of any exact notation of what and how I should play." The narrator mentions Ella Fitzgerald as an influence, who was "...one of the foremost practitioners of the form of talking shit known as scatting. With the air as her scratch pad she has scribbled much syllabic salad into song." The protagonist also makes reference to his aunt (based on one of my own) who, when arguing with her husband, used a difficult-to-decipher slang called "Tut" and inserted it into her opposition to him. And in keeping with the transgressive lingo of "Tut," the narrator, at the end of the introduction, says, "Like all of the rest before me I seem doomed to dissonance and thoughts like highwater pants that are too far from where they're supposed to be."

Ironically, I wrote all this after the novel was completed, which could not have been written while I was discovering what I was writing and how it would sound. I was then persuaded to move it to the beginning, since the narrator could only have acquired this greater clarity about his journey once he'd finished telling his story.

The relationship between the inventiveness of Black idiomatic speech and the improvisational impetus of American jazz are the voices in *Tragic Magic* that recount the story of a young Black man coming to terms with definitions of masculinity that have shaped him and persist even after two years in prison for refusing to serve in the armed forces during the war in Vietnam. Although the experiences of the protagonist, Melvin Ellington, mirrored many of my own, I had (to paraphrase artist Ben Shahn) to find a form that would shape my subject matter. And while I possessed some fragments of the story I thought I wanted to tell, I found myself following the approach of jazz great Miles Davis (on his legendary 1959 record *Kind of Blue*) and groundbreaking comedian Richard Pryor, who took a not fully worked out composition or stand-up performance, and riffed on some of their ideas to see where they would lead them.

During the writing of *Tragic Magic* and anything I've written subsequently, I am never without the rejuvenating sounds embodied in the human voice and their equivalent in music. Like any serious writer, I want to be read. But the silence in response to the publication of my novel was, for the most part, out of my control. What I could control, and ultimately of more value to me, are the voices telling me stories that, like Toni Morrison, I want to read. And like her, I continue to try to write them.

—WESLEY BROWN

A FEW WORDS
BEFORE THE GET GO

AS AN INTERN IN the reed section of sound I have been bucking to win the critic's poll as a talent deserving wider recognition. I know all the standards and am particularly adept at playing the immortal "To Get Along, You Go Along." But there are times when in spite of myself I undermine the popular rendition by not playing it as it was written, and flirt with the tragic magic in *If, Maybe, Suppose,* and *Perhaps.* When this happens I flash on my namesake, Duke Ellington, and recall what one of his mentors, Dad Cook, once told him: Learn the rules, then forget them and do it your own way. More than once this advice has subverted my best intentions to go along with the program. So at auditions to enter the fold I get the urge to play against the melody, behind and ahead of the beat, to bend, diminish, and flatten notes, and slip in and out of any exact notation of what and how I should play.

I studied up on my problem and discovered it was quite a common affliction. The legendary New Orleans cornet player Charles "Buddy" Bolden exhibited the same symptoms and was committed to a state hospital in 1907. After a routine examination, a doctor, S. B. Hays, gave his assessment of Bolden's condition.

> Accessible and answers fairly well. Paranoid delusions, also grandiosed. Auditory hallucinations and visual. Talks to self. Much reaction. Picks things off the wall. Tears his clothes.... Looks deteriorated but memory is good.... Has a string of talk that is incoherent. Hears voices of people that bothered him before he came here.... Diagnosis: Dementia praecox, paranoid type.

I went to a chili house in Harlem where it is said that ideas going through boot camp in Charlie Parker's head resulted in his finding a metaphor inside old chord changes that no one had heard before.

> I remember one night before Monroe's I was jamming in a chili house on Seventh Avenue between 139th and 140th. It was December, 1939. Now, I'd been getting bored with stereotyped changes that were being used all the time... and I kept thinking there's bound to be something else. I could hear it sometimes but I couldn't play it. Well, that night, I was working over "Cherokee," and, as I did, I found that by using higher intervals of a chord as a melody line and backing them with appropriately related changes, I could play the thing I'd been hearing. I came alive.
>
> —CHARLIE PARKER

According to those present, Bird's playing started everyone in the joint to jumping giddy and yapping in a strange tongue that emphasized the buzzing sound of the letter Z. It started when someone said—

"Kiss my ass!" And the comeback was—

"That don't make me no nevermind cause eee-it-tiz neee-iz-zot the beee-iz-uuuteee, eee-it-tiz the bee-iz-zoooteee!"

Bird wailed on at the top of the chords, and the Z string rap spread its healing and hurting potential all over Seventh Avenue. Over the years so-called "buzz talk" became the most popular street lingo and the most difficult for outsiders to decipher.

Many dismissed Bird. They said he played jujitsu music and was not only out to lunch but should be fitted for the wrap-around dinner jacket. Before Bird left the scene he produced many moments of improvisational bliss. It is rumored that one night at Birdland he played the standard *You Go to My Head*, and had everyone within the sound of his horn on their knees attempting to entertain other ways of going to someone's head.

Scatology is a branch of science dealing with the diagnosis of dung and other excremental matters of state. Talking shit is a renegade form of scatology developed by people who were fed up with do-do dialogues and created a kind of vocal doodling that suggested other possibilities within the human voice beyond the same old shit.

Ella Fitzgerald has been one of the foremost practitioners of the form of talking shit known as scatting. With the air as her scratch pad, she has scribbled much syllabic salad into song. Once during a concert in Berlin Ella forgot the words to *Mack the Knife*, but bullskated her way through it with some bodacious makeshift palaver. After her performance she was declared the official voice of the Land of Oooh Blah Deee, traveling air mail special and postmarked "from now on."

I have an aunt and uncle who love to go at it. Their battles are reminiscent of the "carving contests" that went on between musicians during the early days of jazz in New Orleans. Once when they were on the outs, my uncle refused to engage my aunt in any verbal slugging. She was so angered by her unanswered challenges that she began badmouthing him in some strange talk she called "Tut." Not knowing what she was saying about him roused my uncle back into combat. Their jam sessions were restored in the best New Orleans tradition, which trumpeter Mutt Carey described as a battle where "if you couldn't blow a man down with your horn, at least you could use it to hit him alongside his head."

Once during a show at the Apollo the headliner tried to chump the audience off by playing bad imitations of the imitators of his own work. But a woman in the balcony wasn't going for it and let him know about it: "All right, now! Let's have some interpretation!"

This type of ensemble playing rises from the streets of my life like a herd of elephants running off at the mouth. A space opens up where I can take my solo. I open up considering a fish 'n chips joint across the street. Now, some folks hold to the notion that fish were made for the dish and let the chips fall where they may. But just maybe, as a side-order argument, fish were made to swim free and let the chips fall where they can best get a play. There I go again. More rowdy blank verse. Like all the rest before me I seem to be doomed to dissonance and thoughts like highwater pants that are too far from where they're supposed to be.

SOME YEARS AGO I was on the subway with a woman I'd taken out. Her name was Tonya. We hadn't known each other very long but with the rocking train nudging us into one another, I was beginning to get a contact high. At the far end of the car the door slid open and a dude came through, moving like a lean sapling in the wind. As luck would have it, he sat directly across from us, and immediately began giving Tonya the once-over. When he had scoped enough he got up and stepped over to where we were. After a short inspection of the subway map above us he leaned down and began whispering into Tonya's ear. I couldn't hear what he was saying, but whatever it was she shook her head to all of it. After the dude whispered his piece and went back to his seat, I wondered what was going on in Tonya's head. Had he insulted her? And if so, did she expect some act of chivalry on my part? The thought made my bones quiver.

The dude started smiling at Tonya again, giving off a lot of sly action around the corners of his mouth. Maybe she felt it wasn't her place to let on that anything was wrong. It was clear to me at that moment that I was neither knight nor noble, so there was no point in even thinking I could put a royal ass-whipping on anybody. Keeping all this in mind I leaned over to her, raising my voice above the roar of the train.

"Let's move to the front of the train. It'll be closer to the exit."

She nodded and we got up, moving unsteadily toward the front car. I looked back and was relieved that the cat was not following us.

"What did that dude on the train say to you?" I asked after we'd gotten off at our stop.

"Oh, nothing. He asked me if I knew how to get to this street, and when I told him I didn't he asked me if I'd give him directions to the street where I lived. I was a little warm at first but it wasn't worth getting excited about."

"I guess I should have done something."

"What could you have done?" Sensing my feelings had been hurt, she said, "I didn't mean that the way it sounded. It's just that because I'm with a man it goes without saying that he's supposed to protect me from all men. I can appreciate that, but sometimes it slips my mind completely and I just go for myself." She giggled, covering her mouth with her hand. "You know, I almost kicked that dude in his family jewels. I caught myself just in time. I guess that wouldn't have made you look too good if I had. I probably would have been angry at you if you had tried to do something because you would've deprived me of the satisfaction. So don't feel bad about not doing anything... Why are you looking at me like that?"

Wasn't that a blip? Here I was feeling I'd done too little on her behalf and she was holding back for fear she'd do too much. I got away from that woman in a hurry. About two years after the incident with Tonya I was called by the United States government to fulfill my military obligations by protecting it against all boogie men, both foreign and domestic. I didn't realize it then, but I owe Tonya a debt of gratitude for hipping me to the fact that if one is going to put his ass on the line, he should be the one to pick the time and place. I said this to the military at the swearing-in ceremony and to the judge right before he sentenced me to three years for refusing induction.

It's now two years later and I've just been released on parole. When the judge sentenced me I immediately began sandbagging myself emotionally against feeling anything. Now that I've left prison I'm not sure how I feel. The fact of my release is still way out in front of its impact on me. An old dude in the joint once told me to keep good news at a distance. Don't believe it till it happens. And even then, walk with suspicious feet. And that's how I played it last week as I took that long walk out the front gate. My heart played Miles Davis doing *Walkin* with all his quick note shifts, double-clutching slurs, and staccato skips. But my head slowed the tempo of my heart, cautioning it to treat freedom as if it had a very short fuse that could blow up in my face at any moment. Standing in the sally port, I waited for my name to be called.

"Ellington, Melvin—74641-158—paroled."

The barred gate slid open, uncaging the skyline.

On the bus from Pennsylvania to New York I thought about all the people I've ever known who were on the case when it came to dipping what was considered up to snuff. But most of them were smothered by the aroma of what they sniffed. Somehow I've survived, passed over perhaps for the sake of the census. So here I am, ready or not: a token black survivor who has never been able to say, like so many of my fellow bronze buckaroos, "I'm a man and a half," and keep a straight face. But maybe that's because for me manhood ain't got nothing to do with fractions.

No sooner did I get off the bus at the Port of Authority than New York began pushing me around. Body traffic from all the arrivals and departures swirled about me. I stood to the side of a newsstand trying to get reoriented to the flow of rapid transit.

"Can I help you?" the man behind the counter asked.

"No, thank you."

"Well, if I can't help you just make sure you don't try to help yourself."

"What are you talking about?"

"Just what I said. And if you can't figure it out that's too bad cause I don't intend to chew my cabbage twice."

I walked away without a word, determined not to let him mess with the good feeling I had about being back in the city so nice they named it twice. "What's happening, home?" I said, waiting for New York to give me five. But the Big Apple rounded on me and didn't give up any skin. "Well, later for you, too, then, chump-ass city," I said to myself and made my way to the E train to Queens. The morning rush hour was over and I got a seat. My eyes settled on tightly drawn faces reminding me of expressions I'd left only a few hours before. Everybody in the car was doing hard time. They seemed to sense that I had just raised from a fall, but their blank faces did not welcome me back. And why should they have? On the streets you do every day of your time. There is no parole, time off for good behavior, or clemency.

I took a bus from the subway station, and as it moved closer to my neighborhood it was evident that very little had changed. The houses were all Xerox copies of double-decker brick pentagons with attics as poop decks topping everything off. Trees and telephone poles were lined up on both sides of the street as in a showdown, and hedges and shrubbery were barbered into stiff bystanders. The most significant change had been the discreet way whites broke camp as the tide brought in waves of black, yellow, brown, and beige people. I must have been about ten when it started. One night I took out the garbage and saw a moving van in front of a friend's house. On my way to school the next morning I realized that Angelo was gone. Whether we shared an ice-cream cone, argued over the rules of a game, or tried to beat the shit out of each other, everything between us was always personal. What bothered me, even then, about his leaving was that our friendship had been taken out of our hands. If we weren't going to see each other anymore, I couldn't see how anyone else could make that decision for us.

And then one day the color scheme of the neighborhood had only one streak of white left: the Cassioni family.

"Daddy, why didn't the Cassionis move like everybody else?" I asked.

"I guess cause they didn't want to."

"Did the other white people move cause we colored?"

"It looks that way."

"Then why don't the Cassionis move, too, then?"

"I guess our bein here don't matter to them."

"Does that mean they like us?"

"It don't have nuthin to do with whether they like us or not. It's just that they don't mind havin colored people live next to them."

"Why not?"

"It just don't bother them, that's all."

This was my initiation into a world where the way people felt about each other didn't necessarily come from personal involvement. Up to this time, my attitudes toward people were formed entirely as a result of having contact with them. The change occurred as I acquired a more sophisticated understanding of the pronouns *we, us, they,* and *them.* I learned that pronouns not only broke up the monotony of continually referring to people by name as proper nouns, but were also convenient in broadening the base of people you could talk knowledgeably about, especially if you didn't know much about them. It was brought to my attention that black and white people had long ago found the use of *we, us, they,* and *them* invaluable in simplifying their attitudes toward one another.

Surprisingly enough, when most of the whites had moved and *we* were left to ourselves I often heard many of my elders, who were the first of our kind in the neighborhood, speaking against *them,* who had come afterward. For some reason, *they* were not as good as *us.* And it was because of *them* that the whites had moved. Although as the whites had said before: it was nothing personal.

As I got older my facility in using *we, us, they,* and *them,* as well as *ours* and *theirs,* improved to the point where if there was a person or an idea that I didn't want to deal with, I could dispel it with a pronoun. The effect was similar to tear gas in that any disturbances mobbing my mind were quickly dispersed.

I still like to speculate about why most of the whites moved out of the neighborhood. The way they hatted up, you'd have thought we were the second coming of the Moors. Maybe it was the Long Island Sound beckoning them toward Nassau County. It could be that the restless spirit of Columbus, in order to redeem his pitiful sense of direction, was urging whites to complete his journey to the East in search of spices and fabric. Quiet as it's kept, that could be the reason why so many blacks follow whites wherever they move. It's a well-known fact that we have a heavy jones for highly seasoned foods and fine threads.

I really want to give white folks the benefit of the doubt on the reasons for their vanishing act because it would be a drag if they split just to get away from, as the song goes, *we* people who are darker than blue. It's too bad about them, if that's why they moved. And shame on black folks, too, if all the migrating we've done in this world was just to break into the ranks of somebody else's parade. If this is true, we have all become words used in place of ourselves. But I keep forgetting. If in each other's eyes we are simply pronouns, it's nothing personal, since *we* can never know *them.*

The streets were pretty much deserted. I walked past the houses of people I knew and wondered how they were doing. I was particularly interested in what the women were doing. Since I wasn't going with anyone when I was sentenced, my fantasies were impartial as I considered what it would be like to fuck all the women I knew. By the time I reached my block my cock collar had grown to the size of a turtleneck sweater. I hadn't told my folks what time I'd be getting into New York. I didn't want them taking off from work to meet me when I arrived. I needed some time to be by myself, so I wrote telling them to leave the key with a neighbor.

"What is it?" Mrs. Cotton asked through a partially cracked door.

"Mrs. Cotton, it's me—Melvin Ellington. My folks said I could pick up my keys from you."

"Oh, it's you, Melvin. Can't see too good without my glasses. Come on in here and let me have a look at you... You look about the same to me, Melvin. Only difference is you grown now."

"That's what everybody tells me."

"Well, tell me what you been doing with yourself. I haven't seen you in ages."

"I've been away for a while, but I guess I'm back to stay now."

"Thought about what you gonna do?"

"No, not yet."

"Well, Melvin, just remember to do something even if you only spit!"

"I will, Mrs. Cotton."

I wondered if Mrs. Cotton knew where I'd been. Even if she did she would never have mentioned it. She was not a person who visited the business of others unless invited. And she never judged. Instead, Mrs. Cotton had an unassuming way of forcing you to judge yourself. Leaving the house, I saw that she still had her vegetable garden. It reminded me of growing up watching her in her Brooklyn Dodgers baseball cap squatting over tomatoes, green beans, and cabbage. I respected that patch of earth she took such pains with, but once I allowed myself to be meekly led into temptation by some of my friends who dared me to do the Bristol stomp on it. And from behind the bushes we waited for Mrs. Cotton to come home. When she finally turned the corner carrying two shopping bags, we marked time to see how long it would take her to acknowledge the desecration. She stopped and a deep breath welled up within her. But she held it, and then very slowly forced it back to a proper distribution throughout her body. It was as if she realized that the release of all that energy through her nostrils was too much to give up for something as common as a senseless act of destruction.

Instead Mrs. Cotton saved herself for the task of replanting her vegetables.

But guilt whipped me to a fare-thee-well. It was a battle between the fear of the thumbs-down bad finger from the crowd, and the counter-punching shock from within when, as Ray Charles says, I saw what playing to the grandstand did to my song.

"You need any help, Miz Cotton?"

She turned from her work and looked up at me with eyes that knew what brought me to her and the price I'd paid on the way. So Mrs. Cotton did not levy any further duties but allowed me to make restitution in peace.

Recollections such as these are part of the valuables I buried deep within me while I was away. In prison such things could not be left exposed because thieves would definitely break in and steal. But now, for the first time in two years, I was allowing my feelings a ground hog day. Curious but tentative, part of my inner stash peeked the lay of the land. So far so good.

WITH THE EXCEPTION OF a few additional features, the house was as I remembered it. Furniture and order choked every room. My folks have known uncertainty in ways I never have and probably never will. This house was their peace within the confusion of the world around them. My going to jail wasn't easy for them. They always tried to protect me from every conceivable form of Goliath. But, in spite of all they tried to do, I still wound up going one-on-one with the Philistine.

My mother had left a note saying she and my father would be home around six o'clock. I was glad to have the time to myself. I rummaged through some of my old records, looking for sides to fit my mood. I put on *Cowboys to Girls* by The Intruders.

And something in the lyrics stalled me. They reminded me of a time when youngbloods discovered they had cherries to lose and girls got hip to the fruit looming large within them. I wanted to hang tight with my cap pistols and the vacant lot revivals of John Wayne and Randolph Scott Westerns, but the scheming and enticing in the marketplace of puberty had begun. Predictably, my problem was transferring my raw state of mind into word gems that could be put on display in front of girls. Fortunately, my main road dog Otis counseled me on the proper way to go about it.

"You see, what you got to do, Melvin, is learn how to run a game on a broad."

"How do I do that?"

"First you find out if she like you. Like when you in class or in the hall, fool around with her. If all she do is say, 'Stop,' that means you got a chance. If she tells the teacher on you, that means she really digs you and don't care if everybody in class know it. After that, you keep foolin with her till she start foolin with you. And when she do that, you know she want to go with you."

"But how do I ask her to go with me?"

"You get her by herself. Then you tell her how much you dig her and ask her if she goes with anybody. If she say no, then you say, '*If* I asked you to go with me what would you say?' But you got to remember to say *if* cause if she say no, your cool won't be blown."

I made my first move at the movies: the testing ground for copping feels and heavy macking. There were about ten of us in the orchestra section. Everybody was coupled off. I was with a girl named Pearl. I took a few side glances at those around me and saw every dude with at least an arm around the girl he was with. I looked at Pearl. She was slouched in her seat with her left arm propped on the right that straddled her stomach. She was looking directly at the screen, and her left hand muzzled her mouth. I raised my right arm, making like I was scratching my neck, and with a quick jerk brought my elbow down on the back of the seat. I left my arm there for a minute and then slid it down behind my seat and slowly brought it up around the back of hers. I was sweating like a champ! Working my arm off the back of Pearl's seat, I put it around her shoulder. I gave my hand a little swing and it began to move like a pendulum. On about the twenty-third swing my pooped hand grazed her blouse and nudged what I believed was her fledgling right breast. Good Golly Miss Molly! I'd felt her tit and she didn't pitch a fit! So, having succeeded in feeling her knob, I was confident she would let me open the door.

On the following Monday after school I followed Pearl home. Keeping back a safe distance, I waited until all her friends had left her. Then I picked up my pace and when I got to within earshot I called out to her.

"Pearl!"

She stopped and turned around.

"Could I talk to you for a minute?"

"What you wanna talk about?"

"Well, I, ah, been wantin to talk to you for a long time to tell you I dig you a whole lot and I wanted to know if you go with anybody."

"No, I don't go with anybody."

"Well, if you don't, I wanted to know would you go with me?" The words were out of my mouth before I could retrieve

them and insert the safety catch onto the proposition. So I was
O.D.—out dere—falling with no ace in the hole I'd landed in.
  "No!"
  "Why not?"
  "Cause I don't like you."
  "But, Pearl, didn't you feel what I did?"
  "Feel what?

The needle stuck at the end of the record. I was beginning to
feel very musty. What I needed was a shower to wash off the
bus ride from Pennsylvania. I let the heat from the water fill the
bathroom with a good head of steam before I got in...

I'm in the shower with about five other dudes and find myself
admiring the body of one of them. He is tall, lean, and sick-
le-shaped. The slouch in his shoulders is an indication that very
little has impressed him enough to make him straighten up. His
face interests me most of all. His chin, cheekbones, and nose
have an arrowhead sharpness. His hair, sideburns, and mustache
have been trimmed as evenly as a well-kept lawn. And he is the
color of a skillet broken in by cooking.
    I catch myself, almost forgetting where I am. It's not hip to
be looking at a man that long. I don't think anyone saw me, but
I've got to be more careful. In this place you become what people
advertise about you. At any moment someone may decide you

will make a good piece of merchandise. The word from a self-appointed sponsor will go out declaring how mild, how firm, and how fully-packed you are. However, if the product does not live up to its advance billing, something akin to the F.C.C. goes into action. The product will either deliver on its stated purpose or the sponsor will be dealt with by the inmates for defrauding the prison population. One way or the other, somebody will be getting up off of *something*. When you get right down to it, whether it's on television or in prison, the regularly scheduled program is not as important as the commercial message.

I soap myself and wonder what this attraction to the man in the next stall means. I go into some philosophical skydiving in my head about it being a celebration of the human form in an environment fixated on the deterioration of the body and spirit. But that's bullshit. It's square business that if the dude spots me looking at him he'll take it one of two ways: I'm either an asshole bandit or looking to be held up by one.

I try not to draw attention to myself by averting my eyes whenever they rest on him longer than a glance.

"Hey, blood," he says, "why you jerking your head like that for? I know you ain't no Elgin Baylor." We both have a good laugh. I shouldn't have been so uptight about where my eyes wandered. Nobody is paying me any mind. They're too busy indulging in a favorite shower-room pastime: comparing the size of each other's Swanson Johnson. According to penis mythology, black dudes are supposed to have long banana clip johnsons, while white dudes sport drawed-up pee shooters.

"It's them big dicks that get you black guys in trouble," a white dude says. "I bet when you file your income tax you got to claim it as a dependent."

"Don't worry about it," a black counters. "Time has just about run out on you whiteys. When Martin Luther King said, 'How long, not long,' he wasn't just talking about your futures!"

It goes on in that vein and then shifts with black and white screaming on each other for failing to live up to their images. Steam rages in the shower room, and the talk is of the final comedown in the test of manhood between black and white being determined by the one who can get his rizz-od as hizz-ard as a rizz-ock at a mizz-oments nizz-otice.

The water turned cold and I shivered out of my reflections. As I dried off I felt dazed in a time lag, trying to play catch-up with my change in status, but unable to extricate myself from being a prison issue.

On the dresser in my sister's room was a photograph of her taken about ten years before when she was eighteen. Debra had left home around that time and in rapid succession was married and divorced. She had been shacking up with a man for the past few years and my folks didn't dig it. Straightened black hair surrounded her face like a partially drawn curtain. A frown tugged at the left corner of her mouth. She was tilted back on her heels, her left hand cocked on her hip with the elbow out, shotgun style. That defiant stance had gotten the drop on many caught half-stepping with her affections. Compared to Debra's, the poses struck by the ladies of liberty and justice don't convince me that they mean what they stand for. But one look at Debra leaves no doubt in my mind that she is definitely about the business of due process.

I recognized the shape of my father's body in his unmade bed. I could almost see him sleeping and hear his snores. And you've never heard such sounds—sounds resembling the heavy breath grunts of buttermilk bottom preachers. And I was one of the captivated without a church home, drawn to the message coming from his nasal passage. My father's sleep was so deep and his snoring so commanding that the Lord would have needed an appointment before tipping up on him to negotiate a loan of a rib. But Pops' quarrel wasn't with the Lord.

"Damn whiteys, buildin a kingdom off a my back!" How many times were those words hammered into his talk? He would get so worked up when he said them that I never dared ask what he meant. Listening to him snore was my way of eavesdropping on what was going on inside him without bugging him. This was much better than talking to him directly because while he slept I could create my own conversation between us, asking questions I might never have put to him otherwise and imagining his answers blown through snores. Pops' body would be a sprawling heap of steady motion as I crawled into bed with him. Under the surveillance of his snoring, I inchwormed up to his double-barreled nostrils. Up close, the full stature of his nose was revealed: an Egyptian pyramid scarred with hieroglyphics. Latching on to its rhythmic pattern I snuggled my nose under his and drew from his breath, letting it mingle with mine. And from the pull and smell of his rest Pops spoke to me, exhaling the whys and wherefores of his life into me. I'd doze for a while, share some sleep with Pops, and tuck myself inside the labor of his soul.

"Damn whiteys, buildin a kingdom off a my back!"

Those catnaps with my father made those words the handle that cranked out my first clear sounds. His snoring was filled with the lingo that a father must pass on to his son if his son is to carry on the family tongue, get a grip on his own voice, and not lose himself in babbling.

The presence of my mother overtook me as I remembered how some mornings she would sit at the kitchen table staring into a cup of coffee. In between sips I saw expressions settle on her face that had nothing to do with her being my mother and my father's wife... Maybe after the first sip it was the look of a little girl that sprang into her face, entertaining whatever came into her head. Those creases outlining her cheeks after the second sip could have been the signs of some past ache. And maybe after another taste the acid kickback of coffee caused her face to tremble with what might have been a craving for something she desperately needed but could never find. And when she drained the cup of coffee and all the lines in her face were smoothed out, the smile could have been satisfaction over where she'd traveled between the brim and the dregs of the cup.

Of course, all of this was my imagination, but it was all I had to go on, since Moms and I never discussed these things.

THE HOUSE WAS BEGINNING to cramp the need of my senses to stretch a bit more. I decided to go out and see if I could tease the sky. I left a note saying I'd gotten in and would be back around six. I was tempted to stay in and wait, but that would have been too easy. Moms and Pops would act as if nothing had happened. And Debra would probably act as if everything had. I was still looking forward to seeing everybody. I knew a big fuss would be made over me, and after being away for two years I was definitely ready for that.

School was just letting out, and kids dominated the streets. I passed Otis' house. I hadn't seen him in about four years. We had grown up together and had been real tight. I'd always looked up to Otis as a sort of pentathlon champion because of his ability to perform well in all the main events with girls. He could find them, fool them, feel them, fuck them, and forget them with exceptional agility. We were inseparable, and even though I could never match Otis' exploits I was content to be more a spectator in his life than an actor in mine. After high school we drifted apart. I went to college and Otis went into the Marines. We wrote each other for a while, but then the letters stopped.

I rang the bell, but no one was home. I decided to walk over to Rocky's Bar, my old hangout. Someone there might know where he was. A kid almost knocked me over coming through the gate of my old school. I looked at the high iron gate surrounding the building and the grated wire covering the windows. These security measures reminded me of the day I approached another building that had U.S. Penitentiary chiseled into the brick...

I am among about forty men being led inside the wall. Once inside we strip, give the hacks a peep show up our asses, and change into prison-issue clothing. The hacks take us upstairs. We walk down a long corridor and are sized up by the other inmates. They make catcalls and whistle. But none of this bothers me as much as the howling silence from stares. I have never seen such hard, gritting faces before. And then there are the eyes: eyes that explode in your face, taunt you, crawl over you, make propositions and inquiries, but never ignore you. On this first encounter I try to meet them head-on but I'm forced to look away or drop my head.

About sixty of us are jammed into a dormitory for new arrivals. Everyone has picked his company or chosen to stay by himself. I'm lying on a top bunk reading a book when someone touches my shoulder.

"Everything all right, home?"

I jerk up quickly and see a black dude looking very satisfied with himself. It's as if I had reacted just as he expected. Everything about him, from the way he leans against my bed to the way he smiles, gives me the impression that the last time he'd been caught off guard was when the doctor slapped him on his ass at birth.

"Yeah, I'm all right."

"Look, I don't wanna get in your business but is this your first bit?"

"My first what?"

"Is this the first time you've been in jail?"

"Yeah."

"I figured that. I've done two bits before and I can always tell if someone's never done any time. What you in for?"

"Refusing induction."

"Oh, you one a them draft dodgers. How much time you get?"

"Three years."

"Well, that ain't much time. Why didn't you wanna go in the army? You a pacifist?"

"No. I'm just not about what the army stands for, that's all."

"Are you about what this place stands for?"

"No."

"Then why did you come here? Why didn't you refuse to do your time like you refused induction? I mean, if you really believe what you say, you wouldn't have come here either. Unless you prefer jail to the army."

"I didn't want to come to jail. I just couldn't see splitting."

"So you decided to be a hero, eh?"

"Not really."

"Yeah, I bet... What's your name?"

"Melvin Ellington."

"Well, Mel, I'm Chilly and I'm gonna pull your coat to a few things. First thing is, forget about the street. You in the penitentiary now! Most cats in here is hard. They don't know no other way to be. They been hurt a lot, so the first chance they get to hurt back, they take it. All anyone's got to do is look at you and they can tell you ain't had it rough. You probably been to college and shit. Right? Dudes are gonna resent you, especially when they find out what you in here for."

"Why?"

"They figure that with what you got going for yourself you should a been able to scheme your way out a coming to jail. And since you didn't, all that education you got ain't worth a damn. They figure they got more of a beef with society than you do. They never had the opportunities you had. So you not going along with whitey's program don't cut no slack with them. Cats in here been messed over. And here you come, not a mark on you, lookin just as tender as you wanna be, talkin bout you don't wanna fight in no war. Shheet! To them you no different than a white boy."

"So what am I supposed to do? I can't do anything about the way people think."

"You better start doing something about it, cause if you don't you gonna be punk of the month. Look, I don't care one way or the other. I'm just trying to tell you something for your own good. Dudes will try to give you things and get you involved in a lot of jive conversation… It's all a setup to turn you out. Watch yourself when you take a shower. Don't walk around half nude. And for your own protection, make sure you stay on a top bunk. The main thing is to be a man. If someone comes at you with some silly shit, knock hell out of em. If you get your ass whipped, you get your ass whipped. At least you'll get some respect and dudes will know where you comin from."

From then on, I became very self-conscious and Chilly didn't help the situation any. He was always on me about some mannerism of mine that betrayed something funny. It didn't matter if these things seemed natural to me. I had to avoid being labeled a punk. So I watched the way I ate, held my hands, crossed my legs, and walked.

"Every man got some bitch in him," Chilly said. "Some just got more than others. In here you either check it or let it all hang out."

One afternoon a fight broke out in the laundry room between two blacks. Physically, it was a contest of extremes. One dude was thin to the point of being frail, while the other was taller and very husky. Surprisingly, it was the smaller of the two who was selling the most wolf tickets.

"Come on, man. You said you wanted some ass. Well, come on and fuck me now!"

"I'm gonna see how bad you jump when you ain't got an

audience," the larger dude said, visibly shaken from being louded in front of so many people.

"Unh, unh, man. You got to cop now!" Throwing up his hands, the smaller of the two men began dancing for position and then fired a right-hand punch, catching his man flush on the temple. The hacks moved in quickly to break it up and no other telling blows were landed. Everyone talked about how the youngblood had sucker-punched the big dude and in general made him look bad.

The next morning on my way to the dorm after breakfast I was surprised by an inmate on the stairway as I turned to go up the next landing. The lapels on his khaki jacket were turned up, making his weightlifter's shoulders stand out. His Magic-Shave head and dark glasses gave him a cagey look. He looked like the kind of person capable of slipping under doors and through keyholes.

"What's happenin?" he said.

"Nothing's happening."

"That ain't the wire I got on you. The word is that you sho nuff stuff. Now, I don't wanna disrespect you so I'm comin to you like a man to find out what's what, cause if you do mess around you gonna need someone to take your weight when the vultures come around. If you hook up with me you won't have to worry about nobody fuckin with you."

"I'm not what you're looking for."

"Is Chilly takin your weight?"

"Nobody's taking my weight." I moved to walk past him.

As I did, he pulled me roughly toward him and kissed me on the side of the face. I twisted free of his grasp.

"Look, man, I told you I don't go that way."

I backed away from him but he didn't make another move toward me. He just stood there. I remembered the scene the day before in clothing issue. By the standards of the joint, I hadn't acted in the desired manner. When my response to being kissed got around, there would no longer be any question about what I was. I wonder what it would have taken for me to have fought that dude. My problem remains what it has always been: the inability to turn my aggression into a methodical instrument of destruction. In other words, my violent thing ain't coordinated too tough.

"You in trouble," Chilly said that afternoon in the chow hall.

"What are you talking about?"

"Hey, man, come on. You ain't talkin to your everyday lame. This is Chilly! It's all over the joint how you let Showboat kiss you."

"That's not how it happened."

"It don't make no difference how it happened. All anybody's gonna do is look at you and Showboat. Neither one of you is dead or in the hospital. And there ain't no signs of a struggle on either one of you. That's all they need to know."

It was a long walk to the garbage cans where the trays were emptied. I could feel the heavy wattage being laid on me from the head lamps of dudes in the chow hall. Eyes from every-where took swipes at me. And I could understand why. I had failed to kick ass and take names. And that's the calling card for getting over anywhere and the foundation for all credit. It was amazing how my mind was working. Instead of figuring out ways to protect myself from being ripped off by vultures, I was spending time putting their schemes to crush me into a theoretical framework! I kept on walking... but I didn't drop my head. Instead, I stared right through the gauntlet of eyes.

"Ellington!" I looked up from my book and saw a black man standing beside my bunk. He was the color of a penny that had been around, and his hair a seasoning of salt and pepper. But his eyes were the reason I listened to him. They were a tired wise, smacked with a quiet strength and a knowledge past surprises. His eyes played no games.

"I'm Hardknocks," he said. "I just came by to tell you I know dudes have been trying to move on you, and I liked the way you handled yourself when you walked out the chow hall this afternoon... It was important that you held your head up. Not just for those fools messing with you, but for cats who got other things on their mind. I know what you in here for and I think you for real. And there are dudes in here that need to know there are people like you around. They the ones really checking you out. They figured you'd drop your head but hoped you wouldn't. You see, I had your jacket pulled out the file and if you about what it says on paper you aint' got no business dropping your head when push comes to shove. If you didn't drop it for the judge there's no reason for you to drop it in here... Be what you are. That's what it's all about. If a dude digs men, that's cool.

That ain't the problem. The problem is when your shuffle don't jive with your deal. That's what makes cats wanna rip people off. They hate bullskating in themselves and everybody else.

"Another thing. In the joint, people identify you by the company you keep. If you run with snakes it's assumed you down with what they do. That's why it's better to travel alone, cause you stand or fall on your own terms... I'm talking about the dude you been hanging with. Chilly. He ain't no good. He just like his name. What you do is your business, but hanging out with a dude like that is like having walking pneumonia. He's probably the one who sicked Showboat on you. And that makes him even more dangerous. He doesn't do his own hunting. He gets others to bring down the prey. Then he comes in for the kill.

"That's all I wanted to tell you. I usually don't talk to people unless I feel it's worth my time... Later on, youngblood. I think you'll make it."

I lay in bed for quite a while after Hardknocks had gone. Later that evening Chilly asked me if I wanted to go up to the gym. I told him no. The next day I ate all my meals alone and didn't have any rap for him when he came around. That night while I was making my bed Chilly came over to my bunk with an attitude.

"Hey, Ellington, you been rounding on me. Why?"

"I ain't been rounding on you. I just decided to take your advice."

"What you talking about?"

"I'm talking about carrying my own weight."

"What's that got to do with me?"

"It's got everything to do with you. You pulled my coat to a lot of things, Chilly. But I just realized I was letting you do things for me you had warned me not to let anyone do. So I'm taking your advice and not letting anyone take my weight, including you."

"So you can take care of yourself now, eh?"

"I'm going to try."

"Ain't this a bitch. I'm the one kept these muthafuckas from stickin dick in you and now you gonna round on me."

Heads looked up from the T.V., letter writing, reading, and card playing to check out what was going on. Seeing it was Chilly who was responsible for the commotion, their faces showed disappointment. Consistency of style is very important in prison, and Chilly wasn't staying true to form. He was losing his cool, and in the eyes of those watching was no longer worthy of his name. Chilly sensed the attention he was getting and tried to drum up support for his cause.

"Listen, everybody. I wanna tell you somethin. Brown Sugar here has decided he wants to change up all of a sudden and be a man. In that case, I'm serving notice right now that this punkass muthafucka is wide open. Anybody that wants him can have him cause I ain't frontin for him no more... What you gonna do now, punk?" he said turning back to me. Unfortunately, Chilly had misread his audience. Their disappointment had now turned to annoyance over the way he was suggesting to them something he wasn't prepared to do himself. Chilly had forgotten that dudes in the joint are not impressed by words. They are in jail for doing something, not for talking about it. But Chilly kept on talking.

"If you ain't stuff now, you will be soon. All you need is a little pressure. You just ain't streetwise enough to survive in here. All you know is them books. But you don't know nothing about life. You been babied too much. You was already a punk when you got here, so you might as well come on out and be sho nuff bitch…

"It's too late for you to take your own weight. You should a done that the first day when I walked up and touched you. In the penitentiary a man never lets somebody touch him that he don't know. But you ain't no man!"

I looked unwaveringly at Chilly and he sent back a look of shock and surprise scrambling for some face-saving action. There was more to me than he thought, which he took as meaning there was less of him. I could tell he wanted me to say something that would give him an excuse to hit me. But I didn't make it easy for him. Whatever Chilly had in mind would have to begin with him. And then, as if he were raising his hand to wave to someone, he smashed me hard across the face. I was knocked back against the wall. Out on my feet, I was a stricken sail using its mast for crutches. Chilly stood like a predator, ready to spring for the kill. He really wanted a piece of me. But I wanted no part of him. And then, for some reason, I started laughing. At first there were short breaths from the back of my throat; they built to a big production chuckle and ended with my wheezing and falling exhausted on the bed.

"Hey, Chilly, you better leave that dude alone," someone said. "Anybody that laughs behind gettin the shit slapped out of em definitely ain't dealin with a full deck."

Oddly enough, Chilly must have taken my antics to heart because he didn't mess with me anymore. It's possible that laughing did save my ass, since there is a policy in the joint against fucking with people who act crazy.

ONCE I WAS OUT in the general population, my laughing strategy turned to silence. I was given a job assignment in the laundry room and spent most of my non-working hours in the library reading or in the dorm writing letters. When I wrote to family and friends I tried to maintain the fiction that everything was copacetic. But my handwriting told a different story as the words shivered uncontrollably across the page like the last dash of a chicken whose neck has been wrung.

I avoided any recreation that pitted me against anyone other than myself. I had witnessed too many situations where a physical contest became a matter of life and death. So I chose jogging: an exercise where I could use my breath without the fear that I might lose it on a jive tip...

And from the get go I had no wind at all: my legs blown out after just one lap. But a stack of laps buffered my early fatigue. Soon jogging and doing time shacked up in my sweat. And there was just enough salt in my perspiration for me to get a taste of being down as my body wagged toward a raise from a fall.

Except for Hardknocks, I had very little to say to anyone.

I tried to carry myself in such a way that if anyone fucked with me, they had to be wrong. However, my high-flown moral stance wasn't necessarily a deterrent if someone decided to get down mean and wrong with me for lack of anything better to do.

"Hey, Ellington, come on down to the gym and run a few games. We need a third man," a dude said.

"No, I don't feel like it."

"Come on, man, you ain't doin nuthin."

"Yes, I am. I'm reading."

"You can do that later."

"But I'm doing it now."

His jaws loaded up with rocks until his face was only a stone's throw away from Mount Rushmore.

"Don't ever need anything around me, Ellington," he said.

"Hey, man, I just don't want to play."

"Sooner or later you'll have to. And the longer you wait, the more you'll have to pay. And I ain't talkin about basketball."

It was like I was back at day one, trying to figure out the basic prescription for survival. Before I wasn't enough. Now I was too much.

"You getting too jailwise," Hardknocks warned me.

"What do you mean?"

"You too self-reliant. You should a played ball with those cats."

"I thought you said it's better to stand alone."

"Not all the time. They were just trying to let you know that you all right with them. Dudes don't extend themselves too often. But when they do, they don't dig feeling they been chumped off."

"How come I'm the only one that's got to be careful about hurting people's feelings? What about my feelings?"

"What you feel don't fit into the scheme of this place. And if anybody's gotta make an adjustment, it'll have to be you."

I started hanging out a little bit more. Playing a game of Ping-Pong now and then or watching television. I still kept pretty much to myself, except when I talked to Hardknocks and two other dudes named Cadillac and Shoobbee Doobbee.

Cadillac probably got his name because everything was a big thing with him, especially when he was involved. He had a well-stocked torso with arms and legs for days. When he walked he was a V.I.P. brougham limousine Bogarting its way into two lanes. When negotiating a corner he would slink into a Cleveland lowride going into a wide-ass turn while grinning like the grill on a Fleetwood.

"What you reading?" he asked one day while doubleparked next to my bunk.

"*War and Peace*."

"What's it about?"

"Just about everything."

"Who wrote it?"

"Tolstoy."

"He got anything on the ball?"

"A whole lot."

"What did he do with it?"

"He wrote more books."

"He was one sad muthafucka then. What about you? Is that what you wanna do, too?"

"I don't know. Maybe."

"Then you just as sad as he was... You know what happens to cats like that who don't want no more out a life than understanding? They get an ass-whipping every day of their lives cause that's where their smarts is at... That's the sad part cause most people don't have no understanding at all...

"You know what the trouble with most niggers is? They wanna own a Cadillac instead a bein one! But I want what the Caddy stands for. That's why I'm in the joint now... I bet with all your understanding, you don't even know what you want."

"You're right. I don't. But I'd like to find out without being forced into something I don't want."

"What's there to find out? There's only two kinds of people in the world. Those who do the telling. And those who get told. All you got to do is decide which one you wanna be. And with what you in here for, I figure you should a made up your mind by now. If you don't speed on people, you the one gonna end up getting peed on."

"Don't pay him no mind," Hardknocks said.

"He'd do better payin me some mind than you with your fair-play bullshit."

"You run a Coupe de Ville game, Cadillac, but your mind is strictly Pinto material."

"If that's true, you can bet your shit ain't been mistaken

for meatloaf. You may've been named for them hard knocks you've taken but that don't call for no celebration. They ain't even givin up watches for takin shit no more. But I'm a put in a good word for you, cause with all the time you got in they ought a give you Big Ben."

My nerves had gotten raggedy at the root from listening to them run off at the mouth about what was best for me. They didn't even notice when I left. As usual when the dorm began to get to me, I hightailed it for the music room, where Shoobbee Doobbee would be playing records. I'd first met Shoobbee Doobbee coming out of the projection room after a movie. The room doubled as the place that beamed music to every dormitory and cellblock in the prison. I'd heard other inmates talk about this cat with a heavy jazz jones who supported his habit by shaking his head, tapping his feet, and tampering with the origins of famous jazz standards. The day I met him he was wearing a sun visor, a string of reed mouthpieces around his neck, and a drumstick strapped to his waist. When he spotted me, he came over and said, "Do you know what Miles once said to Coltrane after a recording session?"

"No, I don't."

"He said, 'Man, how come you play so long?' And Trane said, 'It took that long for me to get it all out.' I used to keep it all in and wound up knockkneed in a jive humble... Thanks to jazz my toes don't knock no more. I cold-turkeyed to Bird doin 'Now's the Time,' and hucklebucked out a the spell of heroin. So now I'm stone slewfooted, and I plan on keeping my feet turned out at ten to two and never let them turn back in to twenty after eight."

When I walked into the projection room, Shoobbee Doobbee was leaning back in a swivel chair, deep in thought. A spotlight from the ceiling made a cone shape against the wall. Hundreds of album jackets checkered the walls. The side on the record player sounded like a Thelonious Monk tune.

"What's happening, Shoob?"

"Monk!"

"Is that *Straight, No Chaser*?"

"All day... Listen to that statement... Bwah bwah dee daah, bwah bwah dee daah, bwah bwah dee daah, bwah bwah dee daah... Clear as a glass a water... What's wrong, Ellington? You look like you got some botheration on you."

"I'm all right. I just thought I'd come over here and get a change of pace from all the rap in the dorm."

"I hear you! It's a drag cause most folks never change channels... You ever notice that musicians never do much rappin? Like Miles. He never gets up off too much talk. Everybody and their mama got the ass when Miles started turnin back to audiences durin performances. The lames didn't understand he was payin em a compliment by turnin his back. Miles was sayin, 'You cool with me.' Most a the time Miles never trusted nobody enough to give his back to nuthin but the wall.

"On the other hand, the dude whose name you got talks more shit than a little bit. But he ain't never turned state's evidence on his damnself. Once somebody asked the Duke how he got that scar on his cheek, and he said he got it umpirin a duel between a pink baboon and a three-legged giraffe in the back of a Japanese supermarket in Eastern Turkey."

"You play an instrument, Shoobbee?"

"What the fuck you think I was just doin! Bwah bwah dee daah, bwah bwah dee daah, bwah bwah dee daah, bwah bwah dee daah…"

After listening to Shoobbee Doobbee trade licks with records for a couple of hours, I went back to the dorm. On the way I ran into Chilly. We hadn't spoken to each other since our run-in.

"You may think it's over but it ain't," he said. "You may not have submitted to the draft but you'll submit to a skin graft from a shank. One way or another you gonna spread your cheeks. And I'm hip to your shit, so you can forget that laughing act. You can *act* crazy all you want. But I *am* crazy!"

"Why do you keep fucking with me, Chilly?"

"Cause you need fuckin with and I need to be the one doin the fuckin. And Hardknocks ain't no different. He's a little slower than me but he's sure as shit on the same case."

I walked into the dorm like a staggered boxer, knee-buckling down queer street, and was about to take a mandatory eight-count when someone touched my shoulder. I was stunned. It was the first time anyone had touched me like that since the day Chilly had when I first arrived.

"What's wrong?" Hardknocks asked.

"I just ran into Chilly. The hunt's still on."

"He's bullshitting. He's just tryin to see how you'll react."

"Oh, he is, hunh? Well, does that mean no matter what anybody says in this place the opposite is true?"

"It depends on who it is."

"Well, how the fuck am I supposed to tell who's who? You can't be around all the time to pull my coat. That's unless you've decided to take Chilly's old job."

"Look, Ellington, I know what you going through but don't get an attitude with me. Chilly's the one who threatened you, not me."

"That's right, he did. But like you told me, some people are the opposite from the way they appear."

"Oh, so that's it. Sounds like Chilly put more than one buzz in your ear. I'm sorry you feel that way, Ellington, but if after all this time you believe I ain't no different from Chilly, there ain't nuthin I can do about it."

"Yes, there is. If you can take time hipping me to Chilly, you can hip me to you."

"You remember when I first talked to you, I said I usually don't say anything to anyone unless I feel it's worth my while. Well, I figured you knew without my having to tell you where I was at. I guess we both misjudged you."

"Maybe, but right now the only thing I'm sure of is that there ain't nothing I can be sure of."

"What is it about me that you ain't sure of?"

"What you want."

"I probably want the same things Cadillac talks about and at times the same things Chilly threatened you about. The only difference between them and me is there are limits to what I will do. And that brings us to what you want, Ellington, which is protection."

"That's not true!"

"Oh, it's true enough, especially since you didn't say it was a lie. And there's nuthin wrong with that. Some cats join the Muslims. Others lift weights. But most, like you, find a road dog they can talk and walk with. Don't think I ain't been using you, too. I got a lot a time to do, and since you been here I been doing it off you. And when you leave I'll find someone else to do it off of. So don't feel bad about showing some signs a weakness. Every man in here got some cauliflower in their heart. And don't let nobody fool you. The cats that got the most are those that claim to be something more than just a man."

There was no way I could follow that. And I didn't even want to. It was the kind of solo work that reminded me of Gene Ammons playing *Willow Weep for Me*, without ever making it sound like he's copping a plea.

Being around Hardknocks was like listening to the Count Basie Band doing *April in Paris*. No matter how many times you heard the tune, you just had to hear them do it "one more time."

Chilly never got the chance to stick it to me. He was sent back to court on a writ in another case he was involved in. When he didn't return, the rumor circulated that he went into court with a paper bag over his head and testified against his co-defendants as part of a deal with the district attorney. After the trial he was shipped to Sandstone, a joint in Minnesota where snitchers are sent. A few months later, the word was that Chilly had been stabbed to death in his sleep.

When I had completed half my sentence, I went up before the parole board. I took some advice from Hardknocks along with me on the varieties of truth that will and won't set you free.

"Well, Melvin, your record shows that you've done quite well since you've been here. Do you think that's an accurate assessment of your conduct?"

"If it means I've adjusted to being here, that's true."

"Do you think the time you've spent here has been helpful?"

"I think so."

"In what way?"

"Well, I've had a lot of time to think and I realize now the government was correct in sending me here."

"So your views have changed since you've been here."

"Yes, they have."

"Are you saying that you no longer believe the things you said about the government? That if you had it to do over again you'd serve your country?"

"Yes."

"You aren't just saying that to get paroled, are you?"

"Of course not."

"All right, Ellington, that's all!"

"You made it, didn't you?" Hardknocks asked after the hearing.

"Yeah."

"What I tell you. What date did they give you?"

"September twenty-seventh."

"That's not too bad."

"Hardknocks, how much more time do you have before you go up to the board?"

"I don't have to go to the board. I already have my release date."

"What is it?"

"Continue to expiration."

"How long is that?"

"Six years."

"You never told me what you were in for."

"Don't worry about it. It was a while before anybody told me, either. I never mention it because I don't like spreading rumors. Plus cats in here are just as bad as the parole board. They figure if you paying the price, you must a played the game."

"I'll write you."

"No you won't. And I don't want you to either. I been doin my bit off you. But I got to cut you loose, cause the closer you get to your release date the more you'll be thinking about the outside. With all the time I got, I don't need to be hangin around nobody that's gettin short. So I won't be hangin out with you too much from now on. Just promise me when you get out you'll do what you wanna do your own way and not worry about what people think. Cause once you make up your mind, you your own majority."

I LEFT THE SCHOOL GROUNDS, crossed the street, and walked in the direction of Rocky's Bar. I hadn't gone far when I approached someone I knew. It was Alice Turner. She was still the same butterscotch beauty to the bone. And that healthy mouth of hers was turning me on already: lips that were thick strips of flesh stretched like an arched bow across her face. Growing up, I never thought seriously about getting next to her. She was just too fine and I didn't believe I had enough on the ball. And since all the cats with the heaviest reps were hitting on her all the time, I knew I didn't stand a chance. What surprised me was the way dudes who were supposed to be hip messed over her.

Girls never dug her either. They always thought she had her ass on her shoulders. Alice took the harassment in stride, but this only made her tormentors sharpen their signifying jabs. A group of girls once ganged up on her after school. I stood in the crowd and watched them taunt her. Alice stood silently with her neatly braided hair, pleated skirt, knee socks, penny loafers, and her books hugged tightly against her chest.

"I don't wanna fight," she said.

"You think you too good to fight, eh?"

"No. I just don't wanna fight."

"That's too bad," a girl said and swung at Alice, knocking the books from her arms. Alice reacted with punches in the girl's chest. But the other girls grabbed her from behind and wrestled her to the ground. They began to pull at her clothes, trying to destroy what they wished they had while exposing to boys like myself parts of her body we all thought we were doomed to wonder about. When the girls had finished, they seemed pretty done in by their deed. Alice got to her feet, straightened her clothes, and gathered up her books. As she walked through the crowd, it was clear from the look on her face that we had finally won her over to our belief that she was better than we were.

The closer I got to Alice, the more I could see the change in her. She was still as foxy as ever but her fineness had lost its wild abandon. The daring that was once muscled into her walk had been replaced by a guarded stiffness. She smiled when she realized it was me, but that toothy spread that used to span her face was now hemmed in by the fear of hunters. I could tell that someone had crashed the party going on in her soul. But was the party over?

"How you doing, Alice? It's been a long time."

"It sure has. I'm doing okay. How you been, Mouth? I mean Melvin. I know you don't like anybody calling you that anymore."

"That's all right. Most people around here don't know me by any other name."

"I heard about you being in jail. When did you get out?"

"Today."

"That's good to hear."

"I heard you got married."

"I was, but not anymore. What about you, Melvin? You married yet?"

"No."

"Well, if you ever do, be sure you can make it with yourself before you try to make it with somebody else."

"You see much of the old crowd?"

"Not too much. I just moved back from Jersey a few months ago. If I see anybody it's usually at Rocky's."

"I was just on my way over there. You wanna come and have a drink with me?"

"All right."

Rocky's familiar mellow lighting relaxed me immediately. There were only a few people inside when Alice and I walked in. Midgy, the barmaid, was the only person I knew.

"Hey, Midgy."

"How you doin, girl?"

"What's wrong, Midgy, can't you speak?"

"Mouth! Is that you?"

"Yeah, I think so."

"When you get out?"

"Today."

"Well, that calls for a celebration. You and Alice's first drink is on the house."

*   *   *

"It's funny. I really wanted to talk to you, but now I can't think of anything to say," I said.

"What's there to talk about? You just got out of jail and I just got out of a marriage. We haven't seen each other in a long time, so we're having drinks together. After that we'll go our separate ways and probably won't see each other again for another five years."

"I guess I'm just sentimental."

"Did you know I always dug you, Melvin?"

"You mean to tell me that all this time—"

"That's right."

"But you never said anything."

"Neither did you."

All those years that Alice had been in walking distance I'd never told her how I felt about her to her face. She had probably been around a lot of cats like me who felt she was beyond our reach and refused to allow her to be real for others besides herself.

I felt a tent pitch itself in the crotch of my pants.

"What are you doing tonight?" I asked.

"Look, Melvin, I know you just got out of jail. It's only natural for you to want to hook up with a woman. And I'm probably the first one you've run into."

"That's not the only reason I want to see you."

"I didn't say it was. But I just want you to know that you don't have to convince me that it's not on your mind."

"Damn, Alice, who are you trying to convince, me or yourself?"

"I'm just trying to save both of us a lot of trouble… You see, the mistake I've always made with men was wanting them to convince me that they wanted to do more than just fuck. And the funny thing is that I've met very few men who have really wanted to fuck me. If they had, things probably would have worked out better. Most of them only wanted to fuck themselves."

"You think I'm like that?"

"I don't know. But I'm not going to try to find out."

"Now, ain't this some shit!" I turned in the direction of the voice and saw a huge woman standing a few feet away with the backs of her hands pushing their way into bulging hips. She had probably always been heavy, but had moved way beyond that now. I wondered when she had stopped trying to halt the spiral of weight and decided to let it mount without any resistance. But before I could answer my own question I recognized who she was.

"Yeah, it's me," she said, pushing in next to me in the booth.

"Hey, Pauline," Alice said.

"How you been, Pauline?" I asked.

"I was all right until I saw you two over here lookin like you stuck on each other. Don't tell me after all these years you two got a thing goin on?"

"No, we were just talking."

"Just talkin, hunh? That's a switch for you, ain't it, Mouth?"

"People can change, can't they?"

"No! People can't change! People do a whole lotta shit but they don't change!"

"You think so?"

"Hey, I know so! Look at you two. Now, I don't want to get in your business, Alice, but…"

"Then don't!"

"Now, ain't this some shit! That's just what I'm talkin about. You ain't changed a bit. You still think your shit's gold bullion. And you, Mouth. I heard about you being in jail for not goin in the service. That didn't surprise me none. You always been strange. Things other people just go ahead and do always seem to give you problems. That's how you got the name Mouth. Remember?" Yeah, I remembered.

"I can't wait till we play spin the bottle so I can mack with Reatha."

"Yeah, me, too. I'm gonna be macking with Anita for days."

"Who you gonna mack with, Melvin?"

"I dunno yet."

"Well, whoever it is, you better do it right the first time cause if she don't like it she'll tell everybody and they'll think you got crippled lips."

"You know how to mack, don't you?"

"Yeah."

"How do you do it then?"

"You just hold your mouth a certain way, that's all."

"Aw, man, I bet you ain't never macked with a girl."

"So what! You ain't never done it neither."

"Yes, I have, too. Otis and me both did. You just wasn't around."

We were huddled up tight, all eyes on the bottle lying on its side. A hand reached down, gripped it, and with a flick of the wrist turned the bottleneck into an accusing finger making each of us its victim for an instant before the friction of glass and tile halted all movement. The bottle claimed me and a girl named Loretta. She was a striking deep purple, but what got to me the most about her was her smile. When she spread her lips apart, the upper gums showed like a balcony above the front row of teeth. I closed the door behind us, silencing the shouts urging us on.

"Gone, Melvin, make that mack melt in her mouth!"

Once inside, she stood against the wall with her arms folded. I was a few feet away with my head down, shifting my feet.

"What you waitin for?"

"I'm not waitin for nuthin. I just wanted to make sure you was ready, that's all."

"Well, come on then, if you gonna do somethin."

Taking a deep breath, I lunged at her, forgetting all the tender practice macks on the back of my palm. Surprised by my sudden move, Loretta drew up, bracing herself. My mouth rammed hers and it was bones and teeth meeting in total disregard for lips. We both clapped hands over our mouths. I tried to apologize through my bruised chops, but Loretta had already hatted up out of the room. The laughter from the other room told me I was through, over the hill in mackland after just one step.

"One thing's for sure, Pauline," Alice said, "you haven't changed a bit!"

"You damn right! Why should I? You know, for a long time it really drugged me that I couldn't lose any weight. Then I realized that it was because of my weight that men would joke and kid but never play with me. That's your problem, ain't it, Alice? Men always playin with you! But maybe you like bein played with. Shit! Don't tell me people change.

"You know, I been doing hair at Terry's for quite a while. The finest hussies around come in there. They tell me things they wouldn't dare tell anyone else. They figure they can tell me cause I don't have their problems. Now, ain't that some shit! Their problems come from bein touched. Mine come from not bein touched at all! But you know what? The more I listen to them hussies the more I believe I'm in good shape, cause most of them are just as treacherous as the men they badmouthin. Shit! Don't tell me people change!"

"Have you seen Otis around?" I asked.

"Yeah, he's around."

"How's he doing?"

"He's doin fine as long as he keeps his hands in his pockets."

"What's that supposed to mean?"

"He lost a hand in Vietnam," Alice said.

I shook my head but didn't say anything because I was afraid it wouldn't have sounded sincere. And it wouldn't have been. I felt a malicious pleasure over the news that after all those years of flawless movement through the chippies' playground, Otis finally had a handicap.

"What's he been doing since he got out the service?"

"He's been workin as an engineer at that black radio station in Harlem, WHIP. He's definitely played that no-hand bit to a bust," Pauline said.

"Why do you say it like that?"

"Hey, I'm not knockin it. Shit! Behind what happened to him he should get everythin he can. That's more than I can say for you, Mouth. The only thing you gonna get for your trouble is time served."

"That's cool with me."

"Aw, Mouth, come off that noble bullshit! There ain't no difference between you goin to jail and Otis goin in the service. You both were just tryin to impress somebody."

"At least I didn't lose my hand."

"Yeah, but you might a lost something else and don't know it's missin yet."

"Hey, look, Pauline, who are you to question me?"

"Who are you to think you can't be?"

"Well, I don't want to talk about it anymore. All right?"

"That's fine with me."

"Do you know what hours Otis works? I was by his house earlier but no one was home."

"He works the four-to-twelve shift."

"Where's the station at?"

"It's at 128th and Seventh."

I looked at my watch. It was after six. My folks were probably at home by now.

"I'm gonna split."

"If you want to come," Alice said, "some of us are going to a disco later on at this place downtown called La Magnifique."

"Okay, but I'll have to meet you there. I have to go home and see my folks. Then I want to stop by the radio station and see Otis."

"Well, if you decide to come, it's at Fiftieth and Broadway.

"All right. I'll see you later. Excuse me, Pauline."

"You're excused."

PAULINE HAD REALLY GOTTEN next to me. I didn't want to believe that my only reason for not going into the army was to get attention. I had thought a lot about my motives while I was in prison. Otis had schooled me early in the importance of the sound and not the meaning of words. I had to admit that my beliefs were often shaped by the attention I thought they would get. But something happened once that showed me how believing in something could bring a kind of attention I hadn't bargained for.

I was walking along 125th Street. At the corner of Seventh Avenue a crowd had gathered and was listening to a man speak. He was standing on a milk crate. There wasn't much of him, just a hanger-thin frame on which his clothes were hung. He moved like a torch singer, using his body to make the lyrics of a song do something there were no words for. His mouth was a reckless gash with lethal doses of anger jerking at the edge of his voice. What he was saying must have slipped up on something familiar inside those present because necks were craned forward and attention claimed every face.

There had been some disturbance in the street earlier. The police had moved in to disperse the crowd and arrested a boy who didn't move quickly enough.

"I may be young, but I'm old enough to know that youth ain't never been a reason for gettin away clean…"

Heads nodded in rocking-chair fashion.

"That boy couldn't a been more than thirteen. But they busted him for not movin fast enough. But where was he movin to? And who wasn't it fast enough for?"

"Talk about it!" someone shouted.

"I'm not runnin for nuthin," he said, "and I don't wanna be in charge. I just wanna run this," he said, jabbing his two index fingers into his chest. "But I can't do that if I don't go over to the precinct and see about that kid who didn't move fast enough… Some of you may think messin with the po-leece is like goin barehanded in a brass-knuckle affair. Well, strength ain't always a fat-mouth parade. It can also come on like a hush that even dogs can't pick up on sometimes."

He jumped down off the milk crate and began walking down Seventh Avenue. Almost immediately people began filling in behind him. I joined the procession, and soon it extended the length of the block. I don't really know why I followed him, but I think it had something to do with the way his outrage recomposed itself in a word design that x-rayed his hole cards. It scared the shit out of me that anyone would open up like that in front of strangers. My senses were aroused in a way I'd never experienced before. I wanted more. So like everyone else I latched onto the whirlwind he'd created and rode his guts.

At each comer our ranks swelled, thickening the primer with another coat. The hitting of all those feet on the pavement became a drum roll. When we got to the precinct, some police were waiting on the steps. A beefy one with a chest studded with trinkets that might have been left over from the sale of Manhattan stepped forward.

"What seems to be the trouble?" he asked.

"We wanna know what happened to the boy you arrested," said the man we'd followed.

"Are you speaking for all these people?"

"No, I'm speakin for myself. But we're all here for the same reason."

"He's all right. We're just asking him a few questions."

"We wanna see him."

"Everybody can't come in, but since you seem to be the spokesman, you can come in."

"I'm goin in," he hollered back to us.

"Don't you go in there alone, blood!" someone shouted.

"It's either you or nobody," the policeman said.

"I'll be all right," he assured us and went in.

After about fifteen minutes, the boy came out. A brassy cheer went up as the boy disappeared into the crowd. Everyone began to leave, and I was about to go when I saw the beefy policeman put his hand on our spokesman's shoulder. He nodded to what was said to him and then followed the cop back inside the precinct house. In the jubilation over the boy's release, this went unnoticed.

I waited around after everyone had left to see when he would come out. When he did, it was almost dark. His head was down and his arms were wrapped around him as if he were trying to hold himself together.

"What happened?" I asked as he passed me. He raised his head and looked at me with eyes floating in pools of red.

"I didn't move fast enough," he said.

"Ain't you gonna tell anybody what they did to you?"

"What for?"

"So something can be done about it."

"There's no way to prove it. They beat up on me in a way that don't show."

"But if everybody knew what happened—"

"They know."

"But how? I'm the only one that saw them take you back inside."

"There were others besides you that saw what happened. You just the only one that didn't know what was goin on."

"You knew what they would do?"

"Yeah! I made em look bad. And they didn't dig it. So, in exchange for them cuttin the kid loose, I had to take the ass-whippin he was gonna get."

"But if you knew what was gonna happen, why did you speak up?"

"I didn't intend to. It just happened. Most a the time I don't trouble trouble till trouble troubles me. But this time I just couldn't play it safe."

"But how do you know when not to play it safe?"

"When it happens, you'll know. Just don't let nobody else tell you when... What you lookin at?"

"Your eyes."

"What about em?"

"They're red."

"Well, if you think that's from cryin, you wrong. They red from overflowin! Thanks for lookin out for me, youngblood. Later on."

"The cat should a known better," Otis said, when I told him. "He definitely didn't have no smarts."

"But what he was sayin was true."

"That ain't got nuthin to do with it. Whether it's broads or not, you never let anyone know what's really on your mind. If he had really been slick he would a got somebody else to go inside with the police."

"But if you could a heard him. He was serious. He didn't care about the police."

"Then he got what he deserved. Talkin that political talk is all right when you in school. But you don't be runnin that shit in the street."

"All he did was say what was on his mind."

"And all the police did was put something on his ass! Would you a done what he did?"

"I don't know."

"Shit, you know what you would a done and so did everybody else who was there. That's why he's the only one that got the ass-whippin!'"

A distance had begun to crack between us. Otis still believed he had all the answers. But questions were insinuating themselves into me. I was no longer a ready echo for whatever Otis said. And he was surprised to find that more and more after one of his assertions I would not follow up with a refrain but with a theme of my own. This development in our friendship crescendoed when Otis decided to go into the Marines and I opted for college.

One afternoon during my first semester at City College I was sitting in the snack bar leafing through a textbook.

"Hey, my man, didn't you hear about the meeting?" A billy-goat-faced dude stood over me, going through a grab bag of nervous mannerisms that resembled a third-base coach flashing signs.

"What meeting?" I asked.

"The meeting to discuss what's happening in the South and the ways we can support The Movement. You comin?"

"Yeah, I guess I'll check it out."

"My name's Theodore Sutherland. What's yours?"

"Melvin Ellington."

There were about twenty people in the student lounge, either sprawling in chairs or sitting on the floor. Just about everyone sported the roguey attire of faded dungarees, work shirts, and desert boots. The racial composition was an unequally distributed keyboard favoring treble white over bass black.

Theodore, who was one of the organizers of the meeting, was the first to speak.

"As you know, the purpose of this meeting is to form a group that will be a second front for The Movement in the South. Since the press has been reluctant to publicize the recent bombings in Alabama, we see it as our function to pressure our elected officials in Congress to call for an investigation by the Justice Department of these criminal acts.

"Secondly, we want to begin through weekly workshops to politicize the students of this college to parts of the American profile that they don't see. And finally, in order to raise bail money and other operating expenses for The Movement, we will have parties or what we call 'freedom highs' every Friday night. For those of you who decide to join with us in struggle, you should realize that you are not only doctors but also part of the disease. To explain what I mean, Keith McDermott will rap to you."

A white dude joined Theodore at the front of the room. Long, drawn-out hay dogged his face, except for his eyes, which glared out of his head like dime-sized pieces of sky blue. He stuck his hands in his front pockets up to the knuckles as he spoke, shifting his weight from one leg to the other.

"What Theo means is that serious commitment demands experiencing someone else's pain. I know it's impossible for me to really know what a black man feels. So what I must do is get in touch with the pain that whites historically have been estranged from. Once his pain is my own, there should be such outrage in me that it would require that I do something to alleviate that condition.

"As a preliminary step toward feeling the black man's pain, all whites who wish to work with our group are required to read in one sitting Ralph Ginzburg's *One Hundred Years of Lynching* in the presence of Theo or one of the blacks in our group. This should begin to put you in touch with the pain of black people. Reading the details of each atrocity without stopping will be a test of your commitment to The Movement."

"I'd like to add," Theo broke in, "that blacks who are joining us are required to read the book, too. But without a witness. If you can put this book down after beginning it, you'll have to answer to your own conscience... We'll meet again next week at the same time and discuss your experiences with pain while reading *One Hundred Years of Lynching.*"

I tried to get through the book but couldn't. Reading about one atrocity was enough for me. Far from becoming a redcap for every documented lynching in America over a hundred-year period, the cumulative effect of thousands of lynchings left me with no desire to carry the legacy any farther than my knowledge of what had happened. And I felt guilty about being unable to keep my outrage up to the level of the horrors recounted in the book.

At the next meeting, Theo started off by questioning a white chick whose face played peekaboo behind marble cake hair.

"Were you able to experience pain while reading the book?"

"Yes, I was," she said.

"How did it express itself?"

"I threw up."

"And did you continue reading?"

"Yes."

"Why?"

"I felt if black people could survive those horrible experiences, I could tolerate a bad taste in my mouth long enough to finish the book."

"Are you prepared to do anything else besides throwing up?"

"I know I can't undo what's already been done, but now that I've begun to experience black pain I am ready to be the instrument for whatever is required by The Movement."

"What about being white? How do you intend to deal with the resentment you'll have to face because you're white?"

"I'm willing to do whatever is necessary to change that. And if I can't, I'll just have to accept it."

"I see," Theo said, testing the strength of his patchy beard with a few strong tugs. "Keith, why don't you question one of the brothers?"

Keith scanned the room and dropped his two blue dimes on me.

"Your name's Melvin, isn't it?"

"Yeah."

"Well, what did you experience when you read the book?"

"How come you don't question somebody white?" I asked.

"Because the only way to work out antagonisms between blacks and whites is to confront them. That won't happen if

I talk to whites. By challenging one another we get the disease out in the open. When that happens, we can sort it out and then go about finding a cure."

"And what's the cure?"

"The cure is to use these sessions as outlets for fucked-up attitudes so our political action won't be tainted by contradictions... Now, what did you think about the book?"

"I couldn't finish it."

"Why not?"

"It was too much to take all at one time."

"Did you feel any outrage?"

"At first, but then I didn't feel anything."

"Do you think the reason might be that you don't want to deal with history?"

"What's there to deal with? It's already happened!"

"But you've got to put it in its proper perspective."

"And what is that?"

"Do you know why most people in The Movement don't wear ties?"

"No, I don't."

"Wearing ties is a form of contemporary lynch law. In other words, it's the rope revisited. They are part of the official uniform of oppression, lynching people to stifling jobs and choking their identity. Having this perspective forces us to commit a kind of suicide by murdering our capacity to cop out."

"It also," Theo interjected, "keeps a vigil over our consciousness by not allowing us to become what we despise."

I was impressed. Theo and Keith seemed to have thought it all out, complete with contingency theses to tighten up any snags in their arguments. That night there was a party in the student lounge. I ran into Theo when I got off the subway, and we walked over to the school together.

"How are these parties?" I asked.

"They're probably a little different from the sets you're used to."

"In what way?"

"Well, we call them 'freedom highs' because everybody is supposed to slide their fantasies up under somebody else. If the other person digs it, then they both experience it until they've had enough. And that's a freedom high. It's just a way to get all the bullshit out of our system. If you analyze it, you'll see it's not as fucked-up as it sounds. It's all political."

The student lounge was lit with the red tone of a traffic light on simmer. Everyone seemed to be heeding the light as a signal to slow down, because there was very little movement. *Don't Make Me Over* by Dionne Warwick was playing as people went through what I assumed were forms of freedom high. A black dude and a white broad took turns tracing with their fingers the contours of their bodies. Two women, one black and the other white, moved their hands in a massaging motion through each other's hair. A black cat and a white dude faced each other and traded salvos decrying the other's presence in the human race.

"Hello." It was the peekaboo girl behind all the marble cake. For the first time I got a good look at her. Her vanilla skin adhered so closely to bones in her face that skin and cheekbones seemed about ready to change places.

"Hi," I said.

"You wanna get freedom high?"

"I don't know. I'm not really sure how to go about it."

"Get angry at me."

"You haven't done anything."

"All right, I'll help you... Did you know that when you move you look like you're a walking chicken with your ass picked clean?"

I cracked up.

"You're not supposed to laugh."

"I'm sorry, I couldn't help it," I said.

"Okay, let's try again. Say, *What's the word?*"

"What's the word?"

"Thunderbird! Now say, *Who drinks the most?*"

"Who drinks the most?"

"Colored folks."

"Where'd you hear that?" I asked.

"You mean you never heard that before?"

"No."

"Doesn't it bother you having a white person talk to you like that?"

"Not really. It's only a freedom high, right?"

"Not if you don't act right, it isn't!"

"Now you're getting angry. I thought that's what *I* was supposed to do."

"The way you act no one would ever believe you were oppressed," she said, walking away.

I looked around and noticed Keith talking to a black woman. She wasn't paying much attention to him but was looking in my direction. A mane of thick black wool rose above her forehead like a second story. I acknowledged her look with a nod. She excused herself from Keith and walked over to me.

"You're Melvin, aren't you?"

"Yeah."

"I'm Geneva. Theo has told me a lot about you. He says you're a very quiet dude."

"Yeah, I guess so."

"What made you get involved in The Movement?"

"I don't know... I guess it had something to do with seeing this dude stick up for a kid in front of the police. They let the kid go but beat the dude up. At the time I wondered whether it was such a good idea for the cat to have gotten involved. But then when those little girls got blown up in that church in Alabama, I realized getting involved didn't have anything to do with whether it was a good idea or not."

I couldn't believe what I'd said. Something I had never really understood before was clarified for me at the same moment I tried to explain it to someone else. Geneva's face squinted with curiosity.

"What do you think of this freedom high?" she asked.

"I don't know, but Theo has a way of making just about anything make sense."

"You're right about that. Sometimes I wish he wasn't so good at it."

"Have you known him long?" I asked.

"Long enough to be strung out on him."

"You go to City? I've never seen you around."

"I go to Hunter. I met Theo at a demonstration. We talked. And he made a lot of sense. But lately he hasn't been making any sense. He wants me to make it with Keith as part of this freedom-high business. He thinks if I do, I'll get the fantasy of getting a white man out of my system. The *idea* of sleeping with a white man as an experiment is something I've never thought about. But white women are definitely on Theo's mind. That's why he concocted these freedom highs—so he could rationalize chasing white women by making it a form of political work."

"But don't you think he's right about it being better to live out your fantasies than repressing them?"

"But it's his fantasy, not mine... Look at him over there with that white woman who was talking to you." The woman was transfixed as Theo pointed a menacing finger at her as if it were a gun barrel. "Do you know anything about Gandhi?" Geneva asked.

"Not very much."

"Somebody once asked Gandhi what he thought of Western civilization, and he said he thought it would be a good idea. He didn't say it should be made into anything. Just that it would be a good idea. But Theo seems to think every idea he gets is worth pursuing."

"You sure you're not jealous?"

"You damn straight I am! And you won't hear me saying it's political."

"What you two running off at the mouth about?" Theo said angrily, as he walked over to us.

"We're getting freedom high," Geneva said.

"Don't get smart with me, Geneva. I told you what I wanted you to do."

"If asking me didn't get it, telling me definitely won't."

"You just don't have any understanding. All I'm trying to do is get us to go through some things so we won't fuck over each other later."

"Theo, if you want to fuck white girls, go ahead. But don't tell me who to fuck."

"You just have no sense of history."

"And you've lost all sense of anything else."

Theo leaned forward, apparently on the verge of jumping all over Geneva's case, then eased up, smiled, and walked back over to where the peekaboo girl was sitting. Wetness flickered in Geneva's eyes.

"Do you wanna dance?" I asked. She didn't say anything, but turned to me and let me do the rest.

She was numb to the insinuation that dancing close to some-one usually produces. So we moved, but it wasn't dancing.

"Do you believe that history is everything?" she asked.

"What do you mean?"

"There's this group called the Five Per-Centers, and they

believe only five percent of black people know what's going on. They don't believe in history because it's *his*-story, meaning white folks. Five Per-Centers believe in *my*-story, which is a mystery to most of us. According to them, black folks spend too much time listening to the wrong story."

I didn't know if I'd gotten her full meaning, but if what was going on around us had anything to do with it, mystery didn't stand a chance. People had turned into Lazy Susans, revolving to the touch of curious hands, picking for a taste of something choice. Geneva took two fistfuls of my back as if her mystery depended on it.

The Friday night parties continued, but as the profile of events in the country became more vile, it was difficult to keep up the masquerade that freedom highs served a remedial purpose. Demonstrations, beatings, jailings, bombings, and murders glazed our eyes. Eventually, we used freedom highs as a way to bring our gargoyle side out of hiding and avenge ourselves on any bodies of history that were available.

When Malcolm was killed, a memorial service was held in Lewisohn Stadium. I was one of the few hundred shivering people needing to hear someone say something to loosen the full nelson that Malcolm's death had on us. After the first few speakers, I was still hungry for words that would be around when I needed them. Like those spoken by that dude standing on the milk crate on 125th Street. Words that would linger.

And then Theo spoke. As he worked his face, his scattered beard shifted like an earthquake.

"...Many have asked why Malcolm was killed. The answer to that becomes clear once we understand the things that concerned him in life. He knew that freedom is nothing unless it is dangerous. And it is a source of embarrassment for America that his prescription for a people who have moved from deprivation to realized injustice resides in the Declaration of Independence..."

He was into it, his body doing rope tricks and his hands checking out the air like a lead singer.

"Malcolm was the man we thought we were. He showed us how we are victims of very little law and an excess of order, how law has become congealed injustice, how the existing order only hides the everyday violence against body and spirit, how the machinery of society is greased on the misery of the poor, how powerless conscience appeals to conscienceless power, how moral suasion is bastardized before our eyes, and how everywhere the political structure is fossilized..."

"Wake em up, brother! Wake em up!"

"So having been a witness to this, we should no longer be legally or morally bound to obey laws which we have had no say in shaping and which seek to arrest our struggle... There are those who would counsel us in restraint and in the danger of becoming what we despise. But this is a luxury indulged in by those who do not live the reality of our grievances. I believe Malcolm would agree that you don't talk to a starving man about indigestion. It's only after he's eaten that he concerns himself with the dangers to his health from what or how much he eats!"

"Talk the talk, slaves afraid to live!" Theo had us. And when he pushed, we chimed.

"Those who raise the question of the use of violence seem to forget that the development of American democracy has shown that when its political initiatives fail, the use of violence becomes a logical extension of political policy... But unlike the government, we understand that although violence can be explained, it can never be explained away... And it is the recognition of this distinction that is the difference between a revolutionary who can never be radical, and a radical who can never be revolutionary...

"But Malcolm is dead. And it's important that we ask ourselves what must command the living. Too often we use coming together like this as a kind of moral lightning rod instead of a looking glass. None of us can afford to take refuge in the role of speaker or spectator. We must cease being mere fans of the activity of life and make engagement the substance out of which our lives are made. If we don't do this, we are already at the lip of the grave. That's why this whole proceeding is so inadequate. The words seem to wither away almost as soon as they've been said. Because they're just words..."

We all left the stadium without a word, heeding Theo's admonition not to give up any rap unless it was followed by some political punch. For the next few days I said very little to anyone. And I wasn't alone. Theo had also made an undeclared fast on talking. Especially to whites. He began putting signs on bulletin boards saying WHAT'S WHERE TO TALK ABOUT and DON'T SAY IT, DO IT.

Once Theo and I were sitting in the snack bar and Keith came in.

"What's happening, Theo?" he asked, sitting down.

"Not you."

"Don't freeze me out like this, Theo."

"There ain't nuthin to freeze cause you ain't even there."

"You mean I don't exist?"

"As far as I'm concerned, you don't."

"Look, Theo, I understand things have changed and we can't hang together like we used to. But you can't shut me out of history. I'm still part of the struggle."

"You're not part of mine."

"You know what, Theo, you're still freedom high. But it's all black now. And that's cool with me. But what you don't understand is, I'm struggling for my own freedom, not just yours."

"Do you know what a penny buys, whitey?"

"What do you mean?

"A penny buys a book of matches, muthafucka. So if you really wanna fight for your freedom, make an investment in a book of matches, set yourself on fire, and jump on President Johnson!"

"I'm not ready for that yet, Theo. And I doubt if you are either. You're good at delegating people to make sacrifices you're not willing to make. But your real problem, Theo, is that you've never been able to get over the fact that you pushed Geneva and me together before you changed the rules of freedom high.

And now that you've made the game all black, it fucks you up that she didn't come back to you but decided to stay with me."

Theo was on Keith like an ink spot on Manila bond paper. Before some others and I could pull him off, he had sledged Keith's face into meat sauce. I'd always wondered what had happened to Geneva. I never saw her again after my first freedom high. And Theo never said anything whenever I asked about her.

After the fight with Keith, Theo cultivated an even more sinister "don't-fuck-with-me-honky-cause-I'm-liable-to-have-a-trick-up-my-sleeve-and-take-your-head" look. And I followed suit.

"The Five Per-Centers are right about honky history," Theo said. "You got to admit, though, the whiteys got a good starting team, good bench strength, and solid team defense. Their problem is, they only play for ideas and not for fun. Ideas are cool, but when you take the fun out of ideas like freedom, justice, and the American Way, something thrilling becomes killing. And if the whiteys have their way, life will eventually be like watching a newsreel… That's why we need more mystery—so we can fuck with the standard operational procedure. Make them go for the okey doke and jump Proteus on them on general principle. Our rallying cry should be: Wherever We Are Is Already a Minute Ago."

Theo and I walked around City in hooded black sweat suits, calling ourselves the Blue Monks. Whenever someone white said anything to us, we would either ignore them or create mental brick walls by answering with the names of Thelonious

Monk tunes like *Little Rootie Tootie, Straight, No Chaser, Well, You Needn't, Epistrophy, Off Minor, Ruby, My Dear, Crepuscule with Nellie,* and *'Round Midnight.*

In our senior year at City it was clear that the draft board would not view our Blue Monk status as meeting the criteria for conscientious objection to the Vietnam war on religious grounds. Theo came up with the idea that we form a group that was less bizarre and more broadly based. We called it the "No Vietnamese Ever Called Me a Nigger" Caucus. There was another group called the "Hell No, We Won't Go" Brigade, which was made up of whites who counseled students and nonstudents on ways to resist the draft. Theo said what they were doing was irrelevant, since they held on to their student deferments. We agreed to give up our deferments as an act of solidarity with the brothers who didn't have the opportunity to go to college.

At our first organizational meeting I was surprised to see Geneva standing just inside the door of the lounge. She looked tired, but not from lack of sleep. Lines beneath her eyes like skid marks on asphalt revealed a loss of enthusiasm for playing games of chicken with herself.

"Geneva! How you doing?"

"I'll live. What about you, Melvin?"

"I'm hanging in."

"Yeah, I see. When I heard the name of this group, I just knew you and Theo had something to do with it."

"Have you seen Theo?"

"I saw him, but I'm not freedom high over him anymore."

"Are you still mad at him for what he did to Keith?"

"I'm over that, too."

"How are you and Keith doing?"

"We broke up. Theo thinks it was because of him, which isn't surprising, since he thought he was responsible for bringing Keith and me together in the first place. It never occurred to him that my breakup with Keith might have nothing to do with him."

"What made you come back?" I asked.

"I wanted to see both of you. You're an important part of my life. I have to acknowledge it even though I don't want to repeat it. Especially with Theo. He still doesn't see me as a person. He's hung up on some idea he has about me. This time it's his notion of what a black woman should be... It's like that with him in everything. Even when his ideas are sound, Theo never tests them against any opposition. He's only interested in what's going on in his own head... You don't see him that way, do you?"

"I see what you're saying, Geneva, but Theo has a way of making me understand things even if I can't change them. And this gives me a kind of power that reduces the feeling of being helpless."

"You're not helpless, Melvin. Do you remember at that freedom high when you asked me to dance? You were the freest person there. Everyone else was into terrorism!"

"All I did was ask you to dance."

"But that's what parties are for!"

"All right, can I have your attention?" It was Theo. The lounge had filled, and as I looked at the scowls of those in attendance, most were up to the level of meanness required to give the meeting credibility as serious business.

"The purpose of this meeting," Theo began, "is for black and other Third World students here at City to begin to develop a strategy to move from rhetoric to action. You see, it's not enough to badmouth the system. We must be ready to show by our example that we are prepared to discontinue our participation in its vital functions."

"Criticism is an autobiography," Geneva whispered to me.

"So we of the 'No Vietnamese Ever Called Me a Nigger' Caucus are asking those of you who want to become members to go to the Registrar's office and demand that your student classifications not be sent to the draft board. We see this as a first step in a national move by Third World students to force the Selective Service System to draft us. If we are united and armed with the correct political ideology, there is no way that the demagogic politicians and their cut buddies, the avaricious businessmen, can mess with us. And it's in that spirit that we can tell President Johnson, regarding Vietnam, to pull out like his father should have!"

"Whoooocap!"

"All right!"

"Teach!"

"Wait a minute," someone way in the back said, "I don't

see what good giving up my student deferment will do. The only thing I see happening is me ending up in the service or in jail."

"Melvin," Theo said, "would you update the brother's consciousness?"

"What we are trying to do," I said, stepping forward, "is to heighten the contradictions in the society by forcing the government to use repressive measures against us. By ventilating this aspect of government, we can make people see how the government really operates."

He had now come out into full view. He wasn't much larger than I was. But there was a menacing look behind his thick-lensed glasses that wasn't going to be easily intimidated.

"I don't know about anyone else," he said, "but I came to college to get some skills. And I'm not hardly going to blow my education on some bullshit!"

"But, brother," I said, "with a united front we can raise enough hell to end the draft."

"You can go ahead and raise all the hell you want. I'm going to raise my grade-point average!"

"That's too bad," I said.

"No, it isn't," Theo broke in. "In fact, it's very instructive for the brother to be talking this way because he represents a failure of analysis, and as a result, doesn't understand the politics of escalation."

"And what you don't understand," the dude said, "is if you sneeze, you'll draw a crowd."

"That's the only way to raise the level of consciousness of the people," Theo fired back.

"And lower your damn self into a grave."

"That's the price you pay when you choose to be part of the solution rather than part of the problem."

"I'm the solution to any problems I got."

"Brothers and sisters, what you see before you is an example of a renegade. He's worse than an Uncle Tom cause he ain't acting. He's Gunga Din, which means he's exactly what he appears to be. A Tom can be brought home, but a Gunga Din cannot be reformed. And I hope the sisters are listening because you have an important role in making sure the brothers stay righteous."

I turned to look at Geneva, but she was gone.

"If brothers knew that if they shucked and jived, the sisters wouldn't get up off any cat food, they would get their shit together in a hurry and be putting messages on community bulletin boards documenting their righteous behavior... So I'm glad the brother has exposed himself as a Gunga Din for everyone to see... Now, I'd like to move on to the business of drawing up a petition to present to the Registrar's office."

"Wait a minute, I haven't finished yet," the dude said.

"Yes, you have, my man," Theo said, shooting glances at me and some other cats in the room. We converged on him.

"I'm not goin anywhere. Take your fuckin hands off me... You said the Vietnamese never called you a nigger. Well, I ain't no Vietnamese, NIGGER!"

Theo streaked in a direct route to where we were struggling with the dude. What followed was the spirited rhubarb atmosphere of a baseball game where enough punches are thrown for everyone to work out his frustrations before calmer heads are allowed to prevail.

As a result of the fighting, the "No Vietnamese Ever Called Me a Nigger" Caucus was banned from campus. We never saw the dude who disrupted the meeting again, confirming our belief that he was an agent. I never saw Geneva after that either. Maybe she was an agent too?

With no organization to galvanize the black students, Theo and I continued to play the dozens with America, hoping it would live up to our unflattering portrait. Upon graduation we escalated our strategy to force the Selective Service System into drafting us by writing a letter to the draft board saying if we weren't drafted immediately bumblebees in Mississippi would light out from a donkey's ass and go straight to the brains of the members of the local board, buzz their way in, and bloom. We received our draft notices and tokens in the mail within a matter of weeks, which went a long way toward restoring confidence in our analysis of the system and in our belief that we were a threat to its continued existence.

It was then that the wishbone holding Theo and me together broke under the pressure of what we wanted to come true.

"How long do you think it will take people to understand the significance of our act?" I asked Theo, soon after we'd refused induction.

"I been thinking about that, and I don't think I'm going to wait around to find out."

"Why not?"

"The shit is getting serious out here. Didn't you see in the papers today about Keith?"

"No, what happened?"

"He doused himself with gasoline and was in a crowd of people trying to shake hands with Johnson. A secret serviceman got suspicious and grabbed him. Keith had a lighter or something, because when he was grabbed, he ignited himself and the secret serviceman too. The secret serviceman is in the hospital on the critical list... Keith died from his burns."

"God damn! You think he did that behind what you told him that time?"

"Maybe. But even before that we used to talk about putting our bodies in The Movement to the point where they could be used as weapons."

"Theo, were you serious when you told him to use himself as a weapon?"

"I don't know. But Keith must a thought so. Ain't that a bitch? He did what I said. And I don't even know if I'll do what I say."

"You didn't go into the service."

"Yeah, but... I can't seem to keep up with events anymore. The appropriate response changes every day. It's gonna be hard to follow Keith's act."

"Why try?"

"Cause I don't wanna have it said that I ever let a white dude get the best of me."

"But maybe Geneva was right?"

"About what?"

"About history not being everything."

"It'll do until something better comes along. In the meantime, I'm going underground until I can get some things into focus. I've had my greatest moments of clarity after someone I was close to died. First Malcolm, now Keith. It'll take a little while before I'm ready to inflict a political consequence on America, but when I do it'll be outrageous. And I'll live to tell about it."

Theo wanted me to go with him. When I told him I couldn't, he split and left a note saying HAVING BEEN TREATED EXTREMELY DICTATES THAT WE TAKE EXTREME ACTION. While in prison I read a newspaper account about Theo being one of a group of blacks arrested in connection with a series of fire bombings of Harlem police stations.

Unlike Theo, I didn't recover from my scare with uncertainty so quickly. I had believed with Theo that doubt was a punk half-stepping around self-evident truths. And I was quicker than soon and surer than shit about the shape and point of everything I did. But by the time Keith committed revolutionary suicide my rap was no longer the foil for disorder I once believed it was. In fact, my command of imagery was dribbling way past composure toward a directionless spree. So, being unable to play the political licks put down by Keith and Theo, I laid with what I could play and kept my date in court.

I still couldn't go for Pauline reducing my not going into the army to trying to get attention. Chilly had run the same shit on me in the joint. Geneva was more on the money. I had drained the mystery from my history, and as a result, stripped my life of enchantment, which is a more sincere form of instruction.

I TURNED INTO MY BLOCK and saw the car in the driveway. My hands were sweating. As always with my folks and myself, it was time for the battle of wills. I was suddenly very tired. I climbed the steps slowly and rang the bell.

"Welcome home, son." We embraced, but he got the best of it, putting the crush on me before I had a chance to hug back. Pops was short like me, but packed into his runt of a body was about two hundred pounds of muscle swelling inside his pants legs and shirt.

"Melvin's here!"

"You look like you put on some more weight."

"Yeah, that's from all the starch they were feeding me."

"Would you look at this boy!"

"Don't he look good?"

"He sure do. You remember me, don't you, Melvin? I'm your Aunt Clara."

"I remember you, Aunt Clara."

"How you, Melvin?"

"Fine. How are you, Uncle Arthur?" We shook hands and

he applied his legendary grip, which brought me to my knees for a moment of silent prayer. When he let me up I saw my mother standing on the steps leading upstairs.

She was much taller than my father, which was something that used to make me wonder how they made it in bed. No doubt they had found a way, just like a Watusi and a Pygmy would if they were strung out on each other. I didn't rush to Moms immediately, but took her in slowly, following the flow of her smooth, prune-juice skin from her face, down her long, bony neck to the branches of her collarbone. My mother had the airs of a giraffe. It wasn't that she felt superior. She was.

"I guess you don't see nobody else, hunh?" It was Debra. She seemed to be more the spitting image of my mother than ever, with just enough of her own unruly spray thrown in for good measure.

"Now that Melvin's here, why don't we eat?"

"Wait a minute, Rachel! The boy just got here. I wanna make a toast first." A bottle of champagne was opened and glasses were passed around to everyone. "I'd like to make this toast to Melvin. We're all glad to have you back home, son. So here's hoping you're on your way now and won't stop. And with a name like Ellington, there ain't no way you can fail!"

There it was. The invocation of the name Ellington. My father was an ardent admirer of Duke Ellington. He had collected almost every record Ellington had ever recorded and raised me on the discography. Pops had played pretty good stride piano when he was younger, but an accident to his left hand at the factory where he worked halted his ambition to become a musician. While he didn't push me to become a musician, Pops encouraged me to adopt the style of our namesake in whatever I did. According to my father, this style was embodied in an Ellington tune entitled "Diminuendo and Crescendo in Blue," and was on the album *Ellington at Newport 1956.* Pops interpreted the side as an expression of what it meant to be blue or really laid low and still sky right out of the blue. He believed that since being blue was one of the cardinal colors of existence, the most important part of life was the middle distance, or what happened between the diminuendo and crescendo of the blues.

This statement was developed in a solo by the tenor saxophone player Paul Gonsalves, who played for twenty-seven straight choruses. Pops said that every one of the choruses that Gonsalves played was a reshuffling of the same old same old, and that the significance of creating twenty-seven possibilities for the way things could go down turned everybody's head around to the extent that after listening nobody could say, "Tell me something I don't already know," but would have to say, "Oh, yeah?"

The older I got, the more Pops urged me to follow the Duke Ellington lead, embodied in the twenty-seven-chorus solo by Paul Gonsalves. He drilled into me that life was a continuous jam session. And that it was only by trading choruses with the vamp of the blues that I would ever learn that freedom is staying loose when time is tight.

I sat down to a table that was definitely a dumping ground

for the horn of plenty. The sumptuous spread of meats, vegetables, and freshly baked bread was such a departure from the cut-and-dried grit in prison that for a moment I just feasted on the seasoned steam rising from the table.

"I hope the food tastes all right, Melvin. I cooked all your favorites."

"Everything is really good, Moms."

"Rachel! Is that all you gonna put on his plate?"

"He can get more if he wants it, Walter."

"Here, Melvin, take a piece of this country ham."

"No thanks, Pops."

"What's wrong? Why don't you want any ham?"

"I stopped eating pork while I was away." Jaws locked in the middle of chews.

"Why'd you do that?"

"It didn't agree with me, so I stopped eating it."

"It agreed with you all right before you left."

"Well, I just don't eat it anymore."

"Melvin! You aren't a Muslim, are you?"

"No, Moms, I'm not a Muslim."

"Well, I don't know who you been talkin to," Pops said, "but I can't understand bein all choosy about what you eat. I guess you gonna tell me next that you don't eat no flesh period, and that you done joined some group that eats plants and chews weeds all the time."

"It's all right, Walter. If Melvin doesn't want any ham, he doesn't have to eat any." Moms was definitely trying to be slick, playing a vise closing in on me from the other side of the table. Already I was beginning to feel guilty. But I hung tough and didn't accompany my folks' harangue in support of hog meat by eating any.

"You shouldn't let Daddy get away with some of the things he says to you," Debra said later when we were alone. She had always been much more of a fighter than I was, resisting any unjustified attempts to bridle her. All through grade school she was one of the few girls whom boys would never harass. She had a reputation for fighting with such ferocity and abandon that even boys who were older were not willing to tangle with her.

"What difference would it have made if I had said something?" I said. "You know how Pops is."

"Yeah, I know how he is. That's why I always let him know what's on my mind." She was still too bony to be so brazen, drilling the air with both pinkies and staring with eyes that stung. "I've been that way," she said, "ever since Daddy took me to the hospital to see Uncle Arthur after he had an operation. It was the first time I ever saw an adult who was weak and powerless. It was the best thing that could have ever happened to me. After that, whenever Daddy tried to intimidate me, it just rolled off my back, cause it was like watching Uncle Arthur laid up in the hospital scared to death but trying to order everybody around. If I knew an adult who was sick, I couldn't wait to visit them, especially if it was a man. That's probably one of the reasons I decided to become a nurse. Seeing people humbled by physical ailments helps me to deal with the arrogance of people who have their health and strength. So now if I cater to a man, it's either cause I want to or cause I'm being well paid. Daddy knows that and doesn't try to tell me what to do anymore. He knows if I wanted to eat veal cutlet through a straw not to say anything to me about it... But anyway, what about you? Are you okay?"

"Yeah, I'm all right."

"I worried about you a lot while you were gone. You've always been so soft-spoken. How did you keep people from messing over you?"

"I just tried to stay out of the way."

"Well, I'm glad you're out of that place... What are you going to do now?"

"Give up masturbation."

"I think you'll come through it all right."

"Coming ain't my problem. What I need is a co-respondent."

"Hey, I wish I could help you, Melvin, but incest just ain't my thing."

"Yeah, I love you, too, sis."

I slipped upstairs to the bathroom to take a piss. When I flushed the toilet there was a knock at the door.

"Who is it?"

"It's your father." When he got all formal like that it was usually the beginning of a long talk.

"I wanna talk to you about somethin."

"What about?"

"Have a seat." Another familiar line. Pops had opened with

those same lines (years before) when he had given me my first supply of prophylactics.

"How old are you, now, Melvin?"

"Fifteen."

"I been noticin your sheets lately and it looks like to me you been havin a lot of wet dreams. So I guess you at the age where you gonna wanna make some of them dreams come true. But what you gotta make sure of is that you protect yourself. You know what I mean?" I nodded that I did.

"Now, I'm gonna give you some protection to use and when you run out just tell me and I'll see that you get some more… Now, you got a lot of these fast-tail girls out here that'll tell you not to use nuthin. But you do like I tell you and use the protection. I'm tellin you this now so you won't be comin to me later about some little girl you done knocked up.

"Have you gotten any yet?" he said, stirring his right index finger into a circle made by the thumb and forefinger of his left hand.

"Unh, unh."

"Well, you got plenty of time. No need to rush things. Now, I'm not sayin you shouldn't get a little piece as soon as you can. I'd rather you do that than lose your nature playin with yourself."

I was so proud when he gave me those first prophylactics that I wore one to school every day for about a month. However, it was a long time before I had cause to use a rubber for any other occasion.

I sat down on the toilet seat and wondered what he was going to give me this time.

"I'm sorry about what happened at the dinner table a while ago. I wasn't tryin to give you a hard time. It's just that your mother spent a lot of time fixin all the things you like and when you said you didn't want it, I kind a saw red for a minute."

"That's okay, Pops."

"But that's not what I wanted to talk about. What I really want to talk about is your plans."

"My plans?"

"Yeah, the future. You've had a little setback, but now it's time to plan your next move so you don't make the same mistake again."

"Mistake! What mistake?"

"What I mean is that you'll be wiser the next time. And since every generation gets weaker and wiser, you got to have your wits about you cause you gettin weaker all the time. I'm not just talkin about you. That goes for me, too. You see, when I was comin up, I could only do what there was time for. And there wasn't time for very much. But my generation had to bide our time so your generation could do the things we were never able to do. And when you can take the time to do what you want, you're much wiser than somebody whose time was never their own. You understand what I'm tryin to tell you?"

"Yeah, I see what you mean. But how does being wise make you weak?"

"That's because whenever things change for the better, people tend to get weaker. You need more strength to want something and not have any way of gettin it anytime soon than you do once you get it. That's why you'll never be as strong as me. It's the same with the whole black race. We're a lot wiser than we was in the past, but we're not as strong."

"What do you mean by strong?"

"Acceptin the fact that you can't always have things your own way all the time."

"I know that, Pops!"

"You may know it now, but two years ago you was so hard-headed nobody could tell you nuthin."

"What are you trying to do, sentence me again? I already did my time, Pops."

"But you wouldn't have had to do any time at all if you hadn't done so much talkin in the raw!"

"You're probably right about that, but I'm not going to *if* myself to death over it. I did what I did. And if I can live with it, so should you!"

"All right. I was just checking to see where you situated. I'm a believer that if you say enough out-of-the-way things to some-body, sooner or later they'll get tired of it and set you straight on which way they're headed... Was it rough in that place?"

"It wasn't too bad."

"Nobody did anything to you, did they?"

"A few tried."

"Well, I'm glad it's over with. I knew you'd be all right. You an Ellington... You goin out later?"

"Yeah."

"Well, before you go, talk to your mother. She wants to talk to you. But you know how she is. She figures you should come to her. She's probably in the kitchen now. Go talk to her."

Everybody seemed to be intent on wearing me down with these one-on-one inquiries into the whereabouts of my psyche. I felt like a reclamation site. And it was only fitting that my mother should be the last of the three-member panel checking me out.

"You need any help, Moms?"

"No, I'm about finished... Melvin, were you telling the truth when you said you weren't a Muslim?"

"I told you I wasn't. Don't you believe me?"

"I just wanted to make sure."

"Why are you so concerned about whether I'm a Muslim or not? Suppose I was?"

"I know you'd never become a Muslim. Your father and I raised you to believe in God."

"The Muslims believe in God. They just call Him Allah, that's all."

"Melvin, there's only one God and He goes by only one name."

"Moms, Allah is Arabic for 'God.'"

"I don't know nuthin about no Arabic but I believe if you gonna serve God you don't mock Him by calling His name in some strange language."

"Are you trying to say that God can only speak English?"

"He speaks English to me."

"But how does He speak to people who don't?"

"I don't know about that. But I do know that this is America. And if you gonna be here you should speak English. God's got better things to do than waste His time trying to figure out the prayers of people who want to deny who they are. If people wanna pray in Arabic they ought to go to Arabia."

"Moms, you don't really believe that, do you?"

"Yes, I do. You may think I'm foolish, Melvin, but if I am it's from what I come from. I ain't never played the fool to something I wasn't familiar with."

"You know, Moms, that's the same attitude the judge had who sentenced me."

"Melvin, how could you compare me with him? He was a stranger. I'm your mother! The only reason you went to jail was because you didn't do what I told you."

"But I didn't want to go into the army."

I could tell from her face that what I wanted didn't matter. She had brought me into the world and discovered that, as quiet as she tried to keep it, the world still found me. And seeing me bruised didn't hurt her half as much as my refusing her protection. The day that I was sentenced, I didn't know if she had heard what the judge had said or just refused to believe it.

"What happened, Melvin? Is it over? Can we go now?"

"I got three years, Moms." Her face splintered and cracked. But she quickly reassembled the pieces and walked up to the judge's bench.

"Your Honor, I'm the mother, and I don't see how you could judge my son without consulting me first. I'm entitled to that. I know he's not perfect. When he was in school, he would cut up in class just like all the other boys. And if there was any disciplining to be done, I did it. So just because he was my son didn't mean I couldn't be firm when I had to be. So, Your Honor, I think I got some jurisdiction here. You can't just take my rights away like that. I'm the mother!"

The judge never said a word, he just got up and left the courtroom without even looking at her. As I was led away by the marshals and the courtroom emptied, she was still making known my affiliation to her.

"You decided what you gonna do now that you're out?"

"Get a job, I guess."

"That's good. I'm glad you're thinking along those lines, Melvin... You didn't tell Miz Cotton where you were, did you?"

"She didn't ask."

"Well, I think it would be a good idea not to tell people anything, even if they do ask."

"Then what should I tell people?"

"Just tell them you've been away."

"But that's not the truth, Moms!"

"It's not a lie, either."

"Then what is it? You make it sound like I got something to be ashamed of."

"Melvin, you wanna finish drying the rest of these dishes?"

"So do you think I have something to be ashamed of?"

"You know, Melvin, sometimes what people know can hurt you and them, too. What's done is done. You've made your point. There's nothing to be gained by telling people everything. Unless you feel you still have something to prove."

After listening to Moms, I had the strange feeling that I had been washed, dried, and put where I belonged. But I was too tired to care. So I let her reassert herself into the affairs governing my conduct without any protest.

I TOLD MY FOLKS I was going to see Otis at his job and then go to a disco. Debra gave me a ride to the station and I caught the subway into Manhattan. The train pulled in as I bought my token, and I was able to get inside just as the doors closed. The feeling that I was being locked up again gripped me. I was very uneasy and my face must have betrayed that because I noticed a few people staring at me. When I looked back at them, their eyes darted away like peas not wanting to get involved in a shell game. By the time the train reached my stop, the sound of the wheels against the rails had my ears pretty well dummied up. The train made a jerking stop, almost throwing me to the floor. But not forgetting my inmate training, I didn't get uptight. Like the hacks in the joint, the Metropolitan Transit Authority was harassing me, trying to get me to react. But I remained cool and got through the doors just before they closed.

I wondered how it was going to be seeing Otis again. Would he be overly self-conscious about his hand and resent my dropping in on him without warning? In a way I hoped this would be his attitude. He had been such a smooth specimen of manhood that I had to see if the loss of a hand had diminished any of his luster.

At Eighth Avenue a man snapped at me like a cat-o'-ninetails hungry for the taste of flesh.

"*Muhammad Speaks,* brotherman!"

"No, thanks, I speak for myself."

"You're wrong, my brother. You can't speak for yourself until you have submitted to the truth."

"I didn't say I wouldn't submit to the truth. Only the newspaper."

"My brother, *Muhammad Speaks* is the truth!"

"I see."

"No, I don't think you do see, my brother. If you did, you would buy a copy of the paper."

"I'll get one from you some other time."

"Why wait, good brother? The hour is drawing late for the black man."

"I've always been late anyway."

"For a quarter you can find out what it's like to be on time."

"No, that's all right."

"That's the story of the black man in America. Always running from the truth."

"You sure about that?"

"Is pig pork?"

"That's the rumor."

"Brotherman, how long have you been asleep?"

"Oh, ever since you started trying to sell me that newspaper."

"You better wake up, brother. I have a message for you if you'd just open up your dead ears and submit. But you talking like a Negro now. And when you a NeeGrow that means you need to grow!"

"There's probably still some hope for me, then."

He shook his head, dropped away from me, and moved on to someone else.

Farther down the block some sounds scissored into me. Suddenly I found myself in the thick of a knotted ring of kids in front of a record store. They were winding to the sounds like a set of drunken propellers and mimicking the words of the records coming from the outside speakers. And they were together, too, pumping up swift on the balls of their feet, then jabbing their knees out and peddling themselves into a flirtation walk. Every slip in a shoulder, backbone, or hip came off with a stroke of finesse.

Watching them made me wonder about the origin of such dances as the Bop, Philly Dog, Boogaloo, Boston Monkey, Shing-a-ling, Skate, Fat Man, Push and Pull, Funky Chicken, and Penguin. Where did they come from? And how did they spread once they arrived? Maybe a dance is like an idea whose time has come. If it is, maybe it comes into town unawares in the brown bag of a churchgoing woman. And after stealing out of there it shops around for the right body to put the wobble on. And then, before something that was nobody's business becomes everybody's business, the new dance is good news in some unsuspecting soul's muscles and joints.

It struck me that a possible strategy for the race lay in the unpredictable way dances whistle-stop from city to city. If those who had an idea wouldn't tell until it was tapped into their backbones, then it would make more sense to everybody because the idea, like a dance, would be a permanent fixture in their lives. And once someone learned the steps of a new thought, he or she would be a courier for an idea whose time had come.

In keeping with my analysis, watching those kids dance began to trigger movement in me. Having been a child prodigy of Balling the Jack, the Eagle Rock, and the Camel Walk, I was getting the urge to twist out of the everyday run-of-the-mill and flirt with untried orbits.

"Hey, my man," I said, stepping forward, "can I get in on this?"

"Sure, come on and get yourself a step."

So, for a moment, I was a mean rudder knifing through the elements and wasn't to be held in check. But as a quarter-of-a-century-old relic, I didn't want to blow the hoochie-coochie feeling those kids had cornered. So I made my exit.

Four large illuminated letters spelling WHIP hung vertically alongside the building. From the looks of it, they also seemed to spell out what was responsible for the shape it was in. On the third floor of the walk-up a woman sat at a switchboard behind a glass enclosure.

"May I help you?" she asked.

"I'm here to see Otis Edwards."

"Is he expecting you?"

"No, but I'm a friend of his."

"What's your name?"

"Melvin Ellington."

"He's still in the studio. Why don't you have a seat while I call in and tell him you're here."

"Thank you." A security guard was slouched in a chair reading a newspaper. He gave me the benefit of a brief surveillance and went back to his reading.

"Ain't this a blip!" It was Otis. A shaved head dotted with pores and blending into a ripe plum face stuck out of a red turtleneck shirt. The end of the right sleeve was buttoned neatly across, concealing his nub. He had gotten thicker through the chest and shoulders, but was still tapered off lean from the waist on down.

I got up to greet him, extending my right hand. Realizing he couldn't shake my hand, I clumsily gripped his arm with both hands and smiled weakly.

"How you been, Otis?"

"Ain't no need a kickin, Mouth," he said, obviously enjoying my feeble attempt to appear as though I noticed nothing different about him. "You knew that I lost my hand in the Nam, didn't you?"

"Yeah, it's just that seeing it for the first time is sort of…"

"Well, don't worry about it. You'll get used to it. I have." He probably dug the hell out of acting this scene out with anyone who tried to be natural around him and ended up coming off exactly the opposite. It was small compensation for what he'd lost, but he probably took payback in whatever form it came. "How'd you know where to find me?" he asked.

"I ran into Pauline and Alice at Rocky's and they told me… I hope you don't mind me coming."

"No, I don't mind. I'm glad you came. It's been a long time. Almost six years, ain't it?"

"Yeah, just about."

"What's this I hear about you going to jail for not going in the service?"

"You heard right."

"When you get out?"

"Today."

"Shit! We got to hang out then. It's almost time for me to get off, so lay here a minute while I take care of a few things."

When we got out into the street, there was a group of people at the corner bunched like a skyline near an ashcan. Flames spiraled out of the can before breaking off into smoke. A few feet away a short, chunky man holding a guitar was sitting on a milk crate against the side of a building. He began to play, and his fingers moved over the strings with the delicacy of a daddy-longlegs spider.

"Hey, let's check this out," Otis said. "This cat is always out here playing. He's bad!" Then the man began to sing.

> "I'm a man
> M, man
> A, a child

N, non-spoiled
I'm a man."

The authority with which he sang those lyrics made my skin shiver. When he finished, someone from the huddled group of people took a bag from underneath his coat, pulled out a greasy piece of chicken, and passed the bag around. Barbecue sauce slipped from lips and dripped down chins.

"Excuse my hands," someone said, passing a greasy chicken wing.

"Your hands don't make me no nevermind as long as I get me a piece of this gospel bird."

"Hey, who's got the part that goes over the fence?" The way they ate that chicken told me that they not only shared food but the same abuses and jokes.

"Let's split," Otis said.

"Wait a minute. I want to ask him something." The eyes of those crowded around the ashcan turned to fishhooks as I crashed their private dinner party. He was so engrossed with a piece of chicken that he didn't even notice me. "Excuse me. I want to ask you something about that song you were singing."

"I just sing the song. I don't explain it," he said, and went back to tearing at his piece of chicken.

I was reminded of the comeback for all forms of explaining in prison: Stop crying and do your time. How you did your time was much more important than why you were doing it. As I heard from men who had more than enough time to think about how they would do it—a man has to have something to do. And when he reaches the point where he feels he has nothing to do, he either dies or he kills.

"What was that all about?" Otis asked when I caught up with him.

"I wanted to ask him about the words to that song but he didn't want to rap."

"Yeah, he don't rap to nobody that ain't in his set... Hey, I know this bar we can go to that's right near here. It's called 'Vietnam' and it's owned by some Vietnam vets."

I expected a bar with a name like that to have a particular look or atmosphere. But it didn't. The only thing that struck me about the place was the total absence of women. And the conversation between men seemed to lack the arm-wrestling quality associated with most bar talk.

"So tell me somethin, Mouth."

"There's not much to tell."

"How long were you in the joint?"

"Two years."

"You look like you came out of it all right."

"More or less."

"You know, it's funny the way shit works out. I go in the service. You refuse. I lose a hand and you go to prison. I would a never figured you for something like that. Why'd you do it? Not go in the service, I mean."

"I didn't feel like I had a stake in what the army was doing."

"How did you know if you didn't go?"

"I didn't have to go to know."

"Oh, so I guess that makes me either blind or stupid… Is that why you wanted to see me, to tell me that?"

"Look, Otis, I didn't come over here to throw any shit in your face about the Nam. We go back a long way. And I wanted to see you. It's as simple as that. But you did ask me a question. And I answered it."

"You think I was a fool for going into the Marines, don't you?"

"Hey, come on, Otis, don't play on me like that. It doesn't matter what I think. It's what you think."

"Yeah, well, I sure believed all that war crap we used to see in the movies… You remember the Marine Prayer we used to say all the time?"

"Yeah, I remember it… 'Yea though I walk through the valley of the shadow of death I will fear no evil cause I'm the biggest, baddest muthafucka in the valley!'"

"That Marine Prayer shit didn't work in the Nam though. The Vietnamese are slick. They don't go for all that come-out-and-fight-like-a-man shit. They do their thing on the q.t. A couple of times, the VC snuck into the barracks and shanked some dudes in their sleep, just to show us they could do it. Nobody didn't even know it happened till the next morning. After that shit went down a few times, I said later for all them Halls of Montezuma muthafuckas nuttin up behind bein in the Nam. I still knew I was bad, but the VC wasn't gonna give me no chance to prove it. So me and some other bloods started holding up our arms during mortar attacks. Three hits and you got a purple heart and a one-way ticket home. I figured it was better to bleed for a little while than be dead for good."

"Is that how you lost your hand?"

"Damn, Mouth, what I got to do, piss in your face to let you know it's raining? What do you think?" I wanted to tell him to go fuck himself but I didn't. "So what you got on for tonight?" he asked.

"Alice and Pauline told me about this disco called La Magnifique! I figured I'd check it out."

"So you saw the Queen Bee and the Goodyear Blimp? La Magnifique is a pretty swingin joint. I'll cut you in to some stone freaks. And you won't have no problem gettin over on a sympathy tip once broads find out you ain't had no leg in two years."

"Oh, yeah?"

"Yeah! When I first got back from the war I figured that fuckwise I'd had it. But you'd be surprised how many sympathy fucks I got cause I didn't have no hand. Some broads even got turned on by it. I don't wanna brag, but I think I can do more with my nub than a whole lotta cats do with their dicks. No lie! Here, let me show you." Otis unfastened the buttons on his sleeve, rolled it up, and moved his arm in front of my face. Looking at his thick forearm down to the nub made me think of a huge turkey drumstick.

"Yeah, I see what you mean," I said, uptight by the sight of it.

"You know, ever since I lost my hand I've been having this dream about John Wayne."

"What about him?"

"Well, it starts off with John Wayne riding across the prairie looking for some more of the West to win. He's been going through a lot of changes since he was declared unfit for military service during World War II because of bad knees. So the Duke fulfilled his military obligation in the movies with a cat named Yakima Canutt as his stunt man.

"Now after years of taking the Duke's falls, Yakima gives up stunt riding and starts hanging out at the Department of Interior conferences with the Indians. He whoops and hollers for a fair shake for the Indians so he can get a chance to suck on the peace pipe when it's passed around. The Duke tries to talk Yakima into coming back as his stunt man, but all he gets for his trouble is a contact high.

"So, for the first time, John Wayne has to roam the world without a stunt man while he looks for a place to rest the heels of his boots. He's finally busted trying to storm Alcatraz during the Indian occupation. The presiding judge at the Duke's trial is Iron Eyes Cody, the Indian that cries on those pollution commercials. The Duke is sentenced to the Pacific Ocean and tries to Bogart a ride on the sea. While he's treading water, Woody Strode, the black cat in *Sergeant Rutledge,* paddles by in a canoe singing a blues: 'Everybody wants to go to heaven/but nobody wants to die/Everybody wants to know the reason/but never get past why.'"

"Is that it?"

"Yeah, what do you think it means?"

"I don't know."

"It's all in that blues line. Once you know the reason why shit happens, you shouldn't have to ask the question anymore. It's those John Wayne flicks that fucked me around. And now that I know, it's not about why anymore. It's about how."

"What do you mean by that?"

"What I mean is—fair trade ain't no robbery. And until I do something about those flicks I won't feel I've been compensated for what I lost in the Nam."

"But what can you do?"

"Oh, there's something I can do all right. And I've been thinking about it for a long time. Since I've been working at WHIP, I've gained access to a lot of radio and T.V. stations. There's one T.V. station in particular I can get into whenever I want. It's the one that shows all those old late night movies. And when I found out they had prints of just about all of John Wayne's movies, I decided I was going to destroy them."

"What would be the point of doing that?"

"Isn't this reason enough?" he said, holding up his right arm. "You know, Mouth, you've always asked more questions than me. But that's all you've ever done. You've never learned the how of things. Even going to jail wasn't for doing something but for not doing it. In more ways than fucking, you still ain't lost your cherry yet. And I think tonight is as good a time as any to do something about it. Why don't after we do some partying we go down to that station and fire up the image of John Wayne? That ought to make up some for the two years you lost. How bout it? You been grittin too long, Mouth. It's time you started shittin."

WHILE I LISTENED TO OTIS detail how we would carry out his celluloid caper, I thought about how much I've always been drawn to cats who were sure of *how* to do something and didn't spend too much time on *why*. They are always exciting to watch, especially when they deliver the goods. Unable to make it as a practitioner of *how,* I became one of *why* by default. *Why* type of dudes like myself are not very interesting to watch because, with all our deliberation, we don't appear to be doing very much.

But I wasn't about to change. Too much had happened. I had been through too many schemes of desperation of my own to go for one of Otis'.

While I was in prison, a group of students from a local college came once a month to visit those of us who were conscientious objectors. The fact that I was the only black at the first session I attended was a reminder of the static I got from blacks in the joint who believed refusing induction was something only whites did. At that first meeting all the whites greeted me with a variety of black power handshakes, complete with tricky grips.

"How are you, brother Ellington?" one said. "I'm Jason Rich. I'm a C.O., too."

"How you doing?" I said, shaking his hand and noticing his fingernails were mutilated from biting. His body seemed lost in the bagginess of his khaki shirt and pants. Below his confused display of black hair was a face rioting with bumps from some disturbance going on underneath the skin.

"How much time do you have?" he asked.

"Three years."

"They gave me a nickel. I've already done two years. When I went up before the board, they told me to bring it all. I refuse to do any work because they don't pay a minimum wage. Some of us have been trying to organize the other inmates around that issue. We've had a difficult time trying to relate to the blacks, so when we heard you were here we wanted to get with you as soon as possible."

"Oh, yeah? Why's that?"

"You're one of the few black C.O.'s that's ever been here. And in terms of what we're trying to do, your help would be invaluable."

"How's that?"

"We'd like to use you as a liaison in our work to get the brothers to see the connection between Vietnam and the prison system. We take the position that the Domino Theory must be transferred from Southeast Asia to the penal system in this country. And this can be accomplished by creating as many Atticas as possible."

Hearing that convinced me that Jason's general appearance of neglect was also bound up with his thought processes. "Wasn't one enough?" I asked.

"No. Attica was only the model. In order to heighten the contradictions within the prison system, other prisons must follow Attica's example."

"Are you serious?" I asked, dumfounded, looking at everyone in the room. No one said a word. They all caved in out of deference to Jason. "You expect me to run what you just told me to other blacks in here?"

"Since you're the only black political prisoner here, you could make our position more credible to the brothers."

"I doubt it, since it ain't even credible to me."

"That's too bad. It's sad to see a brother not use his black yoga."

"Black yoga?"

"Yeah, you see, black people have a way of crossing their legs and folding their arms." When he said that, I immediately assumed the position. "It's a kind of natural meditation," he continued, "that gives you a daring that most white people don't have. I believe it comes from knowing that the ground you walk on can become a welcome mat one minute and a deathtrap the next. It gives you a looseness to maneuver, where the less gifted rhythmically would fall."

"All this is new to me. I wasn't aware that blacks had all this power just by going through a few mannerisms."

"Most whites who have become politically aware would

give up their white-skin privilege in a minute for some of your black yoga."

"Oh, so you'd trade all your advantages for some black yoga. Well, if it's as valuable as you say it is, I don't know if that's such a good bargain. I mean, that would make me like you, wouldn't it? Sounds like to me you want the goods without going through the changes that created them. That's why you don't mind letting blacks be in the vanguard, doing the funky robot into the sights of those guards in the gun towers. And I don't blame you. Why should you get wasted if you don't have to? But what you don't understand is that I don't want to be you. I want to be in your place!"

"Wait a minute, Ellington! You're twisting everything around!"

"That's right, but I guess that's some yoga that's a little too black for you."

"LOOK, OTIS," I SAID, finally fed up with all his futile talk of revenge, "I'm not going to start throwing bricks at the penitentiary my first day out of jail."

"All right. You ready to split to La Magnifique?"

"Yeah."

We hailed a cab on Lenox Avenue.

"Fiftieth and Broadway," Otis told the driver. He was as wide around as a beer keg and had a head that sunk between his shoulders as he peered at us with owl eyes.

"I usually don't pick up men who're together at night," he said. "Especially on weekends. I figure on a Friday night a man should be with a woman. Two dudes together this time a night ain't up to no good. They either faggots or tryin to rip somebody off."

"You don't have to worry about us cause we ain't hardly into none a that," Otis said.

"You two look all right but I wanna warn you right now, I'm not gonna stand for a stickup or any freak shit in my cab. So let's be clear about that from the git, cause I'm givin up neither money or bootie!"

"Hey, I can understand that," Otis said. He turned to me.

"You gonna try and cop from Alice?" he asked.

"I don't know. I hadn't really thought about it."

"Don't gimme that shit. Your dick's probably been harder than a desert bone all day. Lemme tell you somethin about Alice, though. That's a strange broad. She's been death on dudes since her marriage broke up. Most cats that hit on her don't even come away with a fantasy. You may end up beating your meat before you get any a that."

"What do you think I've been doing for the last two years?"

"I guess you youngbloods are out to do some serious womanizing," the driver said.

"You got that right!" Otis said.

"Well, what you doing for the women these days?"

"I got em takin much dic-ta-tion!"

"Solid on that! Are they takin it all down?"

"You mean, are they takin it all in, don't you, Pops?"

"All right! I hear you, youngblood! Do you ever go down South with the ladies?"

"Damn sure do. I stays in the Dixie Cup."

"Good to hear that you fess up to bein well traveled. A lotta bloods don't wanna admit they spend a lotta time below the Mason-Dixon line... But tell me this, youngblood, are you built for comfort or for speed?"

"I'm all comfort, Pops, slow but sure on every turntable I'm a spindle for. Everybody calls me L.P. for short."

"You pretty swift with the words, too."

"Hey, my rap always downshifts on Friday cause I steady spends the weekend in the passing gear."

"What about you? I'm talkin to you."

I looked into the rearview mirror when Otis didn't say anything.

"Who, me?"

"Yeah. You don't seem to have too much to say."

"That's because I'm not doing too much to speak of."

"Don't worry about it. Ain't nobody else doin much more than scratchin."

He definitely had that right. It reminded me of a dude in the joint named V.D. who would always ask me to write letters for him.

"Here's a flick of the broad I want to write the letter to," he said.

"She's nice."

"Yeah, she's a friend of Jubilee's woman. I wanted somebody to write to, so before Jubilee split he had his woman get her address for me. At first, writin her was just part of my bit. But then I figured since I was goin up for parole this year, she might be able to do somethin for me. So I put her to the test."

"What did you do?"

"I sent her this card sayin how much I appreciated her writin me. And that I would a sent her some candy but I didn't have enough scratch. So the next letter I got from her had some money in it."

"What do you want me to write?"

"Tell her I got to have those letters from people offerin me jobs for my parole hearin next month. I figure even if I don't get a play from the board, I'll be gettin out in eighteen months anyway. She ain't no star or nuthin, but at least I'll have somebody to lay up with when I get out. I feel kind a sorry for her. She tells me all her problems, and I been tryin to help her get herself together... She sent me some short heist pictures of herself. I showed em around in the dorm and some lowlife muthafucka ripped em off. If I catch the muthafucka that did it, I'm gonna bust his ass. I can't have nobody disrespectin my woman."

"Hey, Ellington, I hope you didn't believe none a that shit V.D. told you," Hardknocks said later.

"Why?"

"Don't you know why everybody calls him V.D.?"

"Unh, unh."

"It's cause he's Very Doubtful. Jubilee never gave him no woman's address. V.D. got a sister who's whipped in the mug and ain't got nuthin better to do than write him letters like she's his woman. All his homies know about it. But they don't say nothin cause they figure if he don't mind makin an ass out a sportin life, then that's his business."

A faraway howling wind kicked up in my ear, became a growl, and then shaped itself into a human voice.

"Come on, Mouth, let's go! What you waitin for?" Otis said.

"Don't worry, youngblood," the driver said. "You'll get over with the ladies. Just remember, if you can't cut the mustard, you can always lick the jar."

LA MAGNIFIQUE WAS BELOW street level in a complex of office buildings. It was strange after two years in rural Pennsylvania to be looking up into an unnaturally grown forest of steel. Once inside, Otis and I were dipped into a color scheme of blues and reds, with strobe lights jabbing white flashes. The manslaughter of trees provided the all-wood decor of the bar, tables, benches, and columns rising to the ceiling. The air was husky with the smell of reefer. Smoke and lights cut through the glut of undulating bodies on the dance floor. The record ended and the voice of a disc jockey came over a loudspeaker.

"Okay, y'all. We gonna stop beating around the bush now and get into the wicked thicket with a little *Jungle Boogie* from Kool and the Gang." The music began again and dancing moves burned a mean path south of the waist. Hips shimmied and backbones turned into gyrating snakes. Legs went frantic. Arms tripped into abracadabra branches and performed tricks. Necks did the camel bend and turtle duck before the side ended with dancers going into a tailspin.

"Okay, groove merchants, now that you've put out your feelers to the person you want to hit on, we gonna change up the pace with a little slow hip shifter by The Escorts called *I'll Be Sweeter Today Than I Was Yesterday*. But before y'all make contact, women: beware of the third leg between bowed legs; and men: watch out for those righteously thrown thighs that have left many a young man circumcised."

"I don't know about you, Mouth, but I'm going to lock up with one of these hammers." Otis moved away from me and into the fray. Accompanying him were a bass guitar, horns, a harp, and then...

Male and female were slung over one another as if they'd been wounded in action, each thinking they were in the arms of a medic. Dudes began to test the spines of women to see how far they would go back. And women, spotting a beanstalk-shaped blood, would get the vibration from his snake charm and curl their way around his body. Hands surveyed their partners' limbs for guidance, and mouths staked out claims in necks.

All this reminded me of my first excursion into the new math, where fingers discovered figures. I saw a woman sitting alone in a corner of the room. I walked over to her and extended my hand.

She looked at my hand and then at me. "No, thank you," she said. This had happened to me many times. With her refusal, my hand was left out there, lost in space, a missile with no place to touch down. In the past I would make a quick recovery and move on to another woman. If I got a nay there too, I would continue asking women to dance; after each refusal I would make like a visiting dignitary, thanking them for making my stay a pleasant one. When I'd had enough, I would snap my fingers, trying to give the impression that I'd just remembered some urgent business, and then make my getaway out of the room. This time I just put my hands in my pockets and stood there with a silly grin on my face.

"Now, ain't this some shit." It was Pauline, with Alice. "Damn, Mouth," Pauline needled, "you standin there like an Indian with reservations. I know you tryin to get yourself together, but you stand in that spot too much longer and somebody's going to mistake you for a coatrack."

"...Before we continue," the disc jockey said, "I'd like to take a brief pause for the cause. And the cause this week for all you up-and-coming freaks is who can come closest to dressing like that baddest bone among the dry, the brittle, and the weary: Slick Swanson, disc jockey for WHIP. Now, we have our spotters on the floor to see who is sportin the meanest threads. And the one who is chosen will be freak for a week, courtesy of WHIP. So profile for a while, y'all, and remember that style is character..."

"How's everybody doin?" Otis asked.

"Hi, Otis," Alice said.

"What's wrong with you, Pauline? Can't you speak?"

"Noddin ain't enough for you?"

"Hey, don't do me any favors."

"You ain't gotta worry about that. If you was on fire, I wouldn't even spit on you!"

"Come on, Alice. Let's dance," he said.

"So how does it feel bein with your ace boon coon?"

"I don't know," I said.

"Well, it shouldn't be too hard for you to become his shadow again."

"Look, Pauline, get off my case, okay?"

"Why should I? Gettin on folks' cases is how I get my cookies. I ain't just heavy. I'm like sight. I'm everywhere you look!"

Pauline had gotten on my last nerve. I found relief in the bathroom. Leaning into the urinal, I wondered if Alice's body had any of the same bends and twists of the trees I watched while I was away to remind me of the shape of a woman's body. If we ever got together, I'd want to watch her in the morning when she yawned, and see her arms pull the skin taut over her bones as her spine buttoned her lengthening back. I'd follow the pit of her arm down as it dipped in at the waist and swayed back into her hips and around her behind. I was treed just by the thought of Alice's shape. I flushed the urinal and realized that my chaser to what went down was an emission of jism juice.

"You all right?" Otis asked.

"Yeah, I'm cool." At the mirror above the sink, I watched Otis tighten up his image: carefully adjusting his shirt collar and going through a series of leaning, ducking, and feinting maneuvers.

"I wanna ask you somethin, Mouth."

"What's that?"

"How did you deal with not gettin any pussy all that time?"

"I jerked off from a political perspective."

"What the fuck's that supposed to mean?"

"Well, I used to think about how much a nut and a nation had in common. And I realized you couldn't have a good one unless you remembered the sensation of almost getting one. So I would go off into a suspended nut, somewhere between almost and being there, and imagine that I was doing the pa-changa, and take one step into coming and then two steps back to almost... I did a lot of jogging, too. But usually after a few laps around the track I'd feel like I was getting down with a woman. When I got my second wind I'd really be fired up. By the time I finished my kick on the last lap, I'd already come in my sweat pants."

"You need to get yourself together. With all that funky hand-jivin between your legs you lucky your brains ain't scrambled no more than they are. I hope you get over with Alice. She ain't half-bad. If it wasn't for you not gettin no nookie in two years, I'd try to cop myself."

"Don't do me no favors."

"Hey, don't get the ass with me, Mouth. You know for yourself that the only reason you've ever been able to get over with a woman in my presence was if I didn't want her. You remember how I used to pull broads. Shit! So just cause I'm minus a wing don't mean I still can't fly!"

I could hear it: a vote of no confidence sucking at his words. I'd been waiting for this. But the scare in his voice didn't make me want to grand on him. Instead, I tried to bail him out.

"Hey, Otis, remember when we used to sing in the bathroom at school?"

His face came up from down in the mouth when I hit second tenor, and he joined me on the note below. We carried on like a pair of ad-libbed splibs, making a mean harmony boomeranging off the bathroom walls. And we were bad enough to have put the glass inside window frames and horn rims on notice to the shattering factor of our doowah.

I DANCED WITH ALICE on the next record. It was slow and our legs were a sneaky alternating current between each other's thighs.

"You come here a lot?" I asked.

"Sometimes."

"By yourself?"

"No. I usually come with Pauline."

"You and Pauline tight?"

"Not really. We both just like to cruise."

"Cruise?"

"You don't know about cruising? It means not buying, just looking, thank you. That way I avoid sleeping with men who run out of cigarettes at three o'clock in the morning and realize they might have to talk."

"Are you cruising tonight?"

"Always," she said, giving me a strong thrust with her thigh.

"What was that all about?"

"Don't worry about it. When it means something, I'll let you know."

"Look, Alice, if you're worried about letting somebody get next to you, all you have to do is let yourself get fat like Pauline and your problems will be over."

She stiffened, closing off the peak between her legs. "What do you want to do, Melvin, dance or lead?"

"Dance."

"Let's sit down then, cause I want you to do both."

Back at the table Pauline was lamping the goings on with some very strong eye contact.

"You leave somethin on me, Mouth?"

"No, I was..."

"I know what you was doin. You always doin with your eyes what you ain't swift enough to do with your hands. I catch you starin at me again and I'll put so much of your business in the street there won't be enough left for you to keep to yourself!"

"Give me some slack, Pauline!"

"You in the wrong store, turkey. I deal in flack!"

"Hey, man, I said I was sorry." It was Otis arguing with someone on the other side of the room.

"Sorry don't shine my shoes," a man hollered back.

"Look, I'm trying to be nice, but if you keep fucking with me, you gonna end up with some extra lip."

"Look, you no-hand muthafucka, you try that shit again and you gonna be all nubs."

"You want some of me, man? Well, come on and get some of this ass-whipping. It's free."

"You gonna have me right now, muthafucka!"

"Stop it, Johnny, please! It doesn't matter!" a woman pleaded.

"Get the fuck off me!"

I finally broke through the crowd surrounding Otis. "Hey, come on, Otis," I said, "what you trying to do?"

"It ain't what I'm trying to do. It's what I'm going to do." He stuck out his lips in the shape of a snout and began to suck air into his lungs. After exhaling several times, he went into some T'ai Chi movements, winding his arms into arcs and pivoting his legs simultaneously left and right.

"All right!" someone shouted.

"Do it!"

"Don't hurt nobody!"

"Yeah, you a stone killer when you fightin the air. But I got somethin for your karate ass!"

Otis said nothing, just stared at his adversary and rocked in a stance of preparation: knees bent slightly, back straight with hips, and behind tucked under.

"Neither one of you is mean," Pauline hollered. "You just want to be seen." The room was spiked by a general outbreak of laughter. Then a whistle blew and the disc jockey chimed in over the microphone:

"Come on, bloods, don't bleed. Remember what the people's champ Muhammad Ali once said: 'Games is only for a little while, but you face and teeth is all your life!'"

"No, unh, unh! I'm not takin this shit! I don't care if he don't have no hand!"

"Please, Johnny, let's go!" the woman said.

"No, unh, unh! I'm not takin this shit! I don't care if he don't have no hand!"

"Please, Johnny, let's go!" the woman pleaded again.

"Bitch!" It was so quick I never saw it, but I heard her face break from the force of his fist. Blood jumped from the woman's mouth into her waiting hands. There were screams, and people moved out of the way to allow the woman room to hit the floor, and for Otis and the dude to scuffle.

In the midst of the fierce clinching and teeth gritting, it was difficult to tell who was doing what, since wrestling has a way of confusing the issue of a rumble.

"You ain't gonna get no reputation off a me," the other dude yelled.

"You better pray for your soul, cause your ass is mine!"

"Unh, unh, you ain't gonna get no reputation off a me!"

"Have your fun, muthafucka, cause I'm gonna have mine in a minute!"

"Ain't this some shit? These lames ain't gonna do nu-thin," Pauline hollered. "All they doin is huggin. They both probably faggots!"

"Hey, you two. They callin the PO-LICE!"

They kicked back from each other with the recoil of a high-powered rifle and contented themselves with calling each other out of their names before things quieted down.

"I know about a party uptown. Wanna go?" Alice asked. We all agreed.

"What happened?" I asked in the cab.

"Aw, the lame got uptight cause I stepped on his shoes."

"Was it on purpose?"

"No, his feet were in the way. He shouldn't a even been with that broad anyway... Yeah, I know what you thinkin. That's why I want to do the thing I told you about. It's just what I need. It'll clean me out... That dude was lucky he came at me in-between moves. I didn't have a chance to get my breathin together."

"Nigger," Pauline said, "if you was as bad as your breath, you would a been able to deal no matter how he came at you."

"Yeah, that's easy to say when you on the sidelines."

"And I ain't never claimed to be nowhere else. You the one grandstandin, not me. And if you talk shit on front street, your ass should be ready to make a public appearance!"

"You keep runnin off at the mouth and my foot's gonna make a public appearance in your ass!"

"Oh, yeah? Try it. And I bet I'll kick you in your balls so hard you'll think it's the World Series!"

THE PARTY WAS IN a multi-terraced highrise on Riverside
Drive overlooking the Hudson River, not too far from the
George Washington Bridge.

"Alice!" a woman screamed, when she opened the door.
"I'm so glad you came, girl!" Her hair was slicked back tight
against her scalp, and her glossy walnut face was meticulously
highlighted with eyeshadow, rouge, and red raspberry lipstick.

"You know I wasn't going to miss your party, Norma. I want
you to meet some friends of mine. This is Pauline, Melvin, and
Otis."

"Hi," she said, flashing a flawless set of gems.

"Hi," we said in unison.

We followed her into a huge apartment of rooms spilling
with people. In each room was a bazaar of different moods and
scenes. I recognized faces I hadn't seen in years. It looked like
a reunion of the old Ivy League set who once wore cardigan
sweaters, desert boots or penny loafers, dug the music of Herbie
Mann and Johnny Pacheco, subscribed to *Esquire* magazine,
went to Coattails on Thursday nights at City College, partied

at the Kappa House, went on the Q boatride every year, and had gone to schools like Central State, Hampton Institute, and Virginia Union. I had always been on the periphery of this crowd, able to crack the ranks in appearance only.

I pushed my way into the room where most of the dancing was going on and was boxed in by a contact high of body heat and song. "I Only Have Eyes for You," an oldie by the Flamingos, had just come on and was causing a stampede of dudes in the direction of all available women.

All the odors of life were alive and well as the room became a gathering of hip-shifting Lonnie Youngbloods and Sassy Shirleys. The stink of laying dead left me, and I could feel myself cooking in the body and the head. I took a deep breath and could tell the difference.

Beep, beep ahhhh
Beep, beep ahhhh
It's in the air
It's everywhere

It was the fire now and I wanted to turn in an alarm for Alice's presence to burn against me. But she had disappeared. So, without a partner, I didn't move, but let the slang from the bodies jostling me take me on a sea cruise.

Otis wasted no time. He had Norma surrounded. And I couldn't pass up an opportunity to eavesdrop on a practitioner of the sly, the slick, and the wicked.

"What you into?" he asked.

"Me," Norma answered.

"You ought to spread yourself."

"I do."

"I mean on something besides yourself."

"No, thanks."

"Don't knock new bread until you've tried it."

"I'm my own sandwich!"

"Yeah, I bet. Two pieces of bread and wish you had some meat."

"And I suppose you're the meat?"

"Government inspected."

"I'll take my chances with a ricochet biscuit."

"You'll go hungry."

"But not for you."

"You're not bad."

"No, I'm better."

"Hey, where you goin?... Oh, you just gonna walk away from me, hunh? You know, you look better goin than comin. Hey, Mouth, check out the ticktock of them buttocks... Well, tell me somethin. What's the digit on Alice?"

"Naught."

"Yeah, I ran a zip myself. Fuck em! They both probably switch-hitters anyway."

"What are you talking about?"

"I can tell just by talkin to that broad Norma that we both lookin for the same thing."

"Bullshit!" I said, walking away.

"Hey, I'm just tellin it like it T-I-S!"

Alice and Norma. Switch-hitters? They couldn't be. But if they were, I wondered which side of the plate they batted on when facing men. I wanted to find Alice but it was almost impossible to move. The crush of people had begun to get to me. I finally found a little more breathing room in the kitchen, where two dudes were talking and smoking a joint.

"Those were some good old times," one said.

"Remember how we used to initiate the new pledgies?" the other said.

"Yeah! What was the line we ran on them?"

"Ahhh... Oh yeah, I remember. We would tell a lame that in order to become a Gentleman of Quality he had to get down with the baddest G.Q. of them all." The joint was passed to me and I took a drag.

"And who was that?" I asked, deciding to get into their game.

"Who are you?" the one who had passed me the joint asked.

"I don't mean to get in your conversation, but I once pledged for the Gentlemen of Quality and I just wanted to know who the baddest G.Q. was."

"He was Peter Prep," he said, giving his friend a conspiratorial glance. But I had something for their asses.

"Where would I have found him?" I asked.

"He was in the Ivy League."

"What position did he play?"

"Okay, my man, since you want to be funny—he played the field!"

"What did he have on?"

"You couldn't miss him. He would be wearing a British casual sky straight out of Scotland, a three-piece herringbone suit, a canary yellow shirt with a maroon tie, a silk maroon hand-kerchief in the breast pocket, and a pair of oxblood cordovans."

"What would I have said had I seen him?"

"You wouldn't have said nothing. You just had to be seen in the spots where he hung out, and sooner or later he would notice that you were bucking for a place among the Gentlemen of Quality. The rest would be up to you. There were a lot of cats who thought they were G.Q.'s, but most of them weren't for real. They may have been gentlemen of quantity, but they weren't gentlemen of quality. Being a G.Q. wasn't a state of mind, my man. It was a fact of life. You didn't decide to be a G.Q. It just happened that way!"

"ORRR-riiiight!" the other dude said, and they both slapped five.

"I hope you didn't mind me having a little fun," I said.

"No, that's all right," said the one who'd done most of the talking. "Were you jiving when you said you pledged for the Gentlemen of Quality?"

"No, I really did."

"Did you make it?"

"No, but I did find Peter Prep."

"Oh, yeah? Where at?"

"It was back in 1964 at the Forty-Second Street Library. I was working in the stacks below the main reading room. And when somebody wanted a book I would send it up on the dumbwaiter. There was always a lot of action in the stacks. Dudes would be steady trying to get next to broads on a studious tip. You could always tell the cats that had the most smarts. They would dress kind of roguey, wear horn-rimmed glasses, look all wild in the eyes and hair, and always carry a beat-up-looking book in their back pocket.

"Now, the baddest dude in the place was a cat everybody called Booksnake cause he read a lot. I knew he was Peter Prep even though he didn't dress according to the description. His game was more together than the card catalogue. When the word got around that Booksnake had a cap, goo-gobs of chicks started inviting him over to their cribs to help them get into their books or whatever else they wanted him to get into.

"After a while, Booksnake began acting very strange. When a request for a book came down to the stacks, he would stare at the slip of paper and say, 'Ask me something I don't already know.' Finally Booksnake's mind locked on him. He not only wasn't working with a full deck, but jokers were running wild in his head. The last time I saw Booksnake, he was in front of the Forty-Second Street Library gangster-slapping one of the lions until his hands looked like chopped liver. I think he's out at Creedmoor now.

"Some people say all that attention went to his head. But that wasn't it. What really happened was that everybody figured

Booksnake had it all, so nobody ever gave him anything. That's what did the job on him... So the moral of this story is: Never get branded as someone who's got it all. If you do, you in trouble."

"Is that true?"

"Well, if it isn't it ought to be," I said.

"You sound like you ain't got it all."

"Who does?" I said.

"Yeah, well, whatever I got I'm taking it out of here and seeing if one of these fine hammers wants any of it!"

"Yeah, bet!" the other dude agreed.

I was fucked up. The smoke had really gotten to me. I moved unsteadily to a room just off the kitchen. Seated were about five or six women, dressed in one continuous wraparound fabric that changed colors as it draped each different one. They seemed cut off from the festive mood in the rest of the apartment, forming a tableau staring at nothing in particular, while listening to a Gloria Lynne record that had just come on.

> Trouble is a man
> a man who loves me
> no more, no more

"Sing the song, Gloria! Sing the song!" one said.
"If it only wasn't so," another chimed in.

> Nothing good to say about him
> Still I hate a day without him

"You chewin my cabbage now, girl!"

Trouble is a man
who's for himself
and that's all

"That's a man's menu all right—me, myself, and I!"

After all we planned
he didn't mean it
Now I understand
I should have seen it

"Go on, Gloria! Sing the shoulda, woulda, coulda blues, girl!"

A man staggered into the room. The platform shoes elevating his heels like staircases were about to cause him to make a crash landing.

"I don't know what you women talkin bout," he said. "I'm Sir Rap a Lot and it's time for me to get a shot at the limelight. I was born in the Dixie Peach but raised in the Big Apple. I'm still fruit but on a different tree. But now nobody can take a bite out a me, you dig. If looks could kill I'd be murder one! Shit! Don't tell me nuthin!"

"Somebody should!" a woman said.

"That's all right. But I know what I'm talkin bout. I'm qualified, you dig. I just had to give up seed for skin. Seed for skin. Trouble is a man, eh? So what! What you broads want me to do about it, throw up?"

"Yeah, if that'll shut you up!"

"All right, I will!" His throat groaned but he clapped his hand over his mouth and wobbled away.

My head throbbed. I tried moving but it was too late.

"Just a minute. Don't leave us so soon," one of the women said. "We'd like to hear from another male man. We've heard from Sir Rap a Lot, but since he had some difficulty talking with his mouth full of whatever he was trying to say, maybe you'd like to speak on the topic of Trouble Is a Man!"

"I'm not in it," I said.

"But you've already been picked. And there's always a chance that if you chew your cabbage slick enough, one of us might be willing to relieve you of some of that sweet batter we know you got backed up in you."

"Come on, sweetie, tell us what your menu is!" They were ganging up on me.

"What do you think about the shoulda, woulda, coulda blues?"

"Have you given up all your seed for skin?"

"All right," I said, "if you really want to know—for me trouble ain't a man; it's my hand, cause for the last two years I've given up seed for foreskin and come away with a very tender groin!"

"Uh-oh, the male man is gettin an attitude."

"That's right," I said. "So what are you gonna do? Cause I'm ready to fuck or fight. But I'm not gonna listen to any more of this shit about your claims to pain!"

I expected a comeback and was surprised when none came. I found my way into the next room and saw Pauline sitting by herself in a corner. When she saw me, her puffy cheeks slackened and their fullness drained down into her jaws. I wondered at what point she started believing that she wasn't too much of nothing and not enough of anything. Maybe never having been asked to dance had something to do with it. But as the saying goes: If you dance to the music, you got to pay to the piper. Ask your mama.

"I haven't seen you since we got here," I said.

"You'll get over it," she said.

"What is it, Pauline? You got a beef with me or something?"

"You givin yourself too much credit, Mouth. I don't get that excited about nobody. Not since I was a little girl and asked my mama to tell me about the world. She spit in my face and said, 'Now you know about the world.' You see that dude over there all wrapped up with that woman?"

"What about them?"

"Look at her eyes. They wide open. Whatever he's doin ain't doin much for her imagination. And she's probably drugged cause she thought if she danced with him, he would take her somewhere. I ain't never expected that from nobody. I remember the day I decided I was in the world as a result of myself, that I wasn't born but was spit from a volcano. And that's the way I like it, cause I don't need nobody's five senses but my own for me to close my eyes."

"Since you're so in touch with your senses, have you seen Alice?"

"It's not my week to watch her."

Fed up, I walked away from Pauline and made my way toward the front door. I was leaning against the wall near the elevator cooling off when Alice came out of the apartment. I liked the way the flow of her bell-bottoms suggested the shape of her legs. And when she swung her arms, the way the mound of her shoulder curved into her upper arm made my skin pebble. And by the time the bell shape of her nose, the proud stones in her cheeks, and her thickly fleshed lips were up in my face, I was hard.

"You looking for me?" she asked.

"I was just wondering where you were. I can only take so much of Otis and Pauline."

"That's good. I saw how you handled those women a little while ago. I was wondering how long you were going to go for their shit."

"I've been wondering how long I'm going to go for yours."

"I can't believe you, Mouth. You're fighting back."

"You like to fight, don't you?"

"Every chance I get. That's why I like Pauline. She fights all the time."

"Yeah, but she ought a lighten up sometimes."

"She only eases up on people who take her on."

"What you thinking about?" I asked after a lull.

"I've been trying to remember how it felt the first time

I went to bed with someone, but I can't. That's probably because I didn't know what I was doing, which was about the way it was the last time I went to bed with someone. I don't even remember who either of the people were. What about you, Melvin? Do you remember the first person you had sex with?"

"Yeah. It was with a girl named Marcy Jones. And I didn't know what I was doing either. Do you remember her?"

"Yeah."

"I was about seventeen and I invited her over my house during the Easter break. So she comes over and I put on some sides. I tried to be slick and put on The Heartbeats. *You're a Thousand Miles Away.* Well, before I had a chance to close the gap, Marcy grabs my hand and says, 'Let's dance.' We finally ended up in my bedroom but I didn't feel like I had anything to do with it. I knew I was a slow starter but it didn't look like she was going to allow me to participate in the activity at all. I was just a hitchhiker going along for the ride but never getting a chance to drive. That wasn't my idea of the way to lose my cherry."

"You're lucky, Melvin. Most men have never experienced the other side of the 'Wham Bam, Thank You Mam.'"

"Oh, yeah? What's that?"

"The Bang Bump, Thank You Chump!"

"Well, I wish somebody would bump this chump off again cause I'd definitely say you're welcome!"

"Oh, so you're one of those men who don't want to do it all by themselves."

"While I was away, an old man once told me, if a woman likes you, she'll let you. But if she loves you, she'll help you.'"

"So?"

"I need help."

"What time is it?" she asked.

"It's almost four."

"You want to come over my place?"

"What?"

"Didn't you hear me the first time?"

"I heard you. It's just that it surprised me. I didn't think you wanted to be bothered."

"I don't mind being bothered. It's getting involved that I worry about."

"Are you afraid of getting involved with me?"

"Yes. Does that surprise you?"

"A little."

"I don't know about you, Melvin. Why can't you accept the fact that I see something in you I like? I don't know which is worse—a man who assumes I want him or someone like you who can't believe I would be interested in him at all. What I'd like from you, Melvin, is a little less opposition. Don't worry. I know what I'm doing."

"I bow to your superior knowledge," I said.

"Why don't we go back inside and tell Pauline and Otis we're leaving."

The congestion in the apartment was beginning to break

up as people left. I didn't have to go far to find Otis. He was pulling on me almost as soon as Alice and I were back inside.

"Where you been, man? I got to talk to you."

"Alice and I are getting ready to split," I said.

"It'll only take a minute, Mouth!" He looked high but there was desperation in his voice.

"You go ahead," Alice said. "I'll go look for Pauline." We went out into the hall and through the door leading to the staircase.

"What do you want to rap about, Otis?"

"It's about those John Wayne flicks I was telling you about."

"Hey, man, I told you I wasn't getting into any of that."

"Look, Mouth, I'm not gonna burn anything up. All I want to do is show you something. It'll only take about an hour."

"Can't we do it some other time?"

"You don't understand, Mouth. I need to do it now. Do you remember Audie Murphy? The cat that got all those medals in World War II? Well, after he got out of the service he slept with a German Luger under his pillow. I didn't understand why until after I got back from the Nam. He was caught up cause he'd been to hell and back. And he found out that a hero ain't nuthin but a sandwich. That's why he started makin movies. That was probably the only thing he felt safe doin. Well, I been hellified, too. And when it really gets bad, like now, seeing those old John Wayne flicks is the only thing that gets me back together. But I don't wanna go by myself tonight. Just come with me for about an hour. Don't worry, you won't blow the pussy."

"Fuck you, Otis! I'm not worried about that. I just don't want to get busted."

"I told you, all I want to do is watch a few film clips."

"I don't see why you'd want to see those flicks anymore after the way they jammed you around."

"What you don't understand is that when losing my hand starts to get to me sometimes, it's because I'm pissed off that the war wasn't like the movies. But once I watch a few John Wayne pictures I'm all right. All I want is an hour of your time, Mouth. An hour!"

Alice and Pauline were waiting in one of the front rooms with their coats on when I came in.

"You want to stop at Wells' for some chicken and waffles?" Alice asked.

"That sounds good. Would it be all right if I met you there?"

"Oh, you have something else planned?"

"No, it's just that Otis is sort of flipped out. He's going through a thing about his hand. I think I ought to stay with him for a while. I'll meet you at Wells' in about an hour."

"Melvin, if you want to get together some other time, that's all right with me."

"Unh, unh! I'll be at Wells' in an hour."

"Would you listen to him?" Pauline said. "Now, ain't this some shit!"

On the way down to the television station I wondered if it was wise to go with Otis, no matter what he'd said. He seemed coherent, but so had Cecil Pendergrass, a black lawyer I'd gone to see before my case came up for trial. He had an office in the Hotel Theresa on 125th Street, and was known for his handling of political cases.

"Come in!" an annoyed voice yelled when I knocked on the door. The office was a wreck of legal books and papers strewn over chairs, desk, and floor. Pendergrass sat behind the desk, almost an oddity amidst the volumes of bound words. White hair rose from his head in one wild shock. He looked at me with two nail heads that almost eclipsed the whites of his eyes. "Yes, what is it?" he asked.

"I was told you take draft cases."

"Are you a draft evader?"

"Yes."

"What's your name?"

"Melvin Ellington."

"Aren't you going to ask me who I am?"

"Well, I assume…"

"Never assume, young man. If you are what you purport to be, I trust you didn't arrive at your conclusions about the armed forces through assumptions. However, in this instance you assumed correctly… and I take it since you came to me you're not going to leave the country but are staying to face the music? Is that correct?"

"Yes, but that was an assumption on your part, too."

"That's what lawyers are trained and paid to do: transform

assumptions into unmitigated fact, which is why people such as yourself seek us out. And now if you're through trying to match wits with me, we can get down to the business at hand."

"All right," I said, securely put in my place.

"Well, as you can see," he said, pointing to photographs on the walls of himself and famous black political figures, "I've represented the spectrum from Malcolm to Rap to Huey... So the only thing I want to be sure of is: Are you prepared to go to jail?"

"Well, I don't want to, but if it comes to that, I will."

"If it comes to that!" he said incredulously. "Look, why don't you tell me the grounds on which you refused induction, because if your position is really an attack on the system, you can forget about any hope of getting off."

"Well, I filed for conscientious-objector status on the grounds that an analysis of America shows that the armed forces are an instrument used to extend the American empire."

"Ahhh, I like that!" he said, leaning back in his swivel chair. "Most of the C.O. cases I've come across have been strictly on moral grounds. But yours has broader political implications. It even parallels an argument I've been developing. Your case could be the opportunity I've been waiting for to launch my thesis."

"How much time do you think I'll get?" I asked.

"Time? Oh, well, depending on how strong my attack on the entire American socioeconomic system is, you could luck out and get the whole five years."

"Luck out?"

"That's right. You see, the political capital gained from being a political prisoner is proportional to the severity of the sentence. Human beings are creatures of extremes and are not given to sympathizing with anyone who has not been given the maximum punishment. Most people will indulge any excess. Whether it's luxury or degradation doesn't make any difference. It all runs together. To paraphrase Martin Luther King, longevity has its place if the sentence you receive is harsh enough to make a political point...

"But let me get to the real business and explain to you the line of argument I'm developing that relates to your case." He searched frantically through the piles of papers on his desk. "Ahhh, here we are," he said, holding a legal-size pad in front of him and leaning into his presentation. "Now, my position is based on a reinterpretation of the rule of law which says a citizen must accept the result of a decision rendered against him, even if he considers it immoral. It's my position that the rule of law represents the interests of a privileged class, which means that not only blacks but most Americans have never been involved in the process of codifying the rules for their security. Concomitantly, the most heinous crimes by America against its own citizens are not represented by laws...

"Let me give you an example. There was a case of a black man from Harlem who was arrested for throwing garbage into the street around the City Hall area. When the police questioned him about it, he said he had volunteered his services to the City of New York as a garbage recycler. When the police tried to humor him by asking how long he'd been on the job, he told them since the anti-litter campaign when Mayor Lindsay came up to Harlem and started things off by picking up the first piece of litter. The mayor then handed the trash to an aide, who handed it to another aide, who passed it on to another, until it ended up in the hands of—you guessed it—our boy, who threw it back out into the street. As a result, he kept on throwing garbage into the street, but only around City Hall. He said he didn't think he was breaking any laws, since he was only trying to keep pace with the garbage the city was handing him...

"He got thirty days, but the point he made was absolutely brilliant. There are laws against littering but none against the conditions of the poor, of which littering is only a symptom. So the rule of law we pay homage to is an abstraction used to divert our attention from the fundamental ills of this society, which that black man was attempting to dramatize by violating the sanctity of the law. Your case is similar, in that your breaking of the law was not directed against other victims but against one of the primary exporters of the American empire—the armed forces...

"Since you'll be going to jail anyway, we should build a case that will get you the most time. So what I'd like you to do is write me a two- or three-page statement of your position and let me do the rest. And if you were willing, I could give you some scenes to act out that are guaranteed to get you a few contempt charges and bound and gagged, Bobby Seale style. How about it?" His bronze face glowed as if he were imbued with not only the revelations from the burning bush, but also from one that had been barbecued. "You don't know how glad I am that you came in. This case could put me back into the front ranks of advocates of lost causes."

"Lost?" I asked in disbelief.

"I mean that figuratively speaking, of course."

I told him I'd be back, but I didn't return, content to take my chances in court as my own advocate. So far, I had been one of the principals in doing myself in. I don't believe I would have ever forgiven myself had I relinquished my top billing in my own undoing for a minor supporting role in Cecil Pendergrass' scenario.

BELOW SAN JUAN HILL between Tenth and Eleventh avenues was the building that housed the film footage on the dominant male image in America for over thirty years.

"The last movie ends about three, so the projectionist should be gone," Otis said, as he opened the door on the side of the building. On a screen in one room an unattended projector showed a fuzzy picture with a scratchy soundtrack.

"What's that?" I asked.

"It's film static. This is what you see when a station goes off the air. The projectionist puts it on when he leaves. It runs for a couple of hours until the station comes back on again. It's weird how they make it. The picture is really a swarm of gnats trapped in a fish tank. The sound is recorded snatches of old Conelrad tests, telephone dial tones, needles sticking at the end of records, rain, and improvised breathing. Once or twice a year they film new static to replace the old. They got hundreds of feet of film just on static alone."

"Get the fuck out a here!"

"If I'm lying, I'm flying."

The film library was a seven-tier, walled-in jungle gym. Each tier had shelves stacked with films in large silver discs. A staircase spiraled through the middle of each tier to the bottom.

"The Westerns and war movies are on the last two levels. Don't talk too loud and don't walk too hard. This place is wired for sound. An alarm system goes off if the walls or floors absorb over a certain number of decibels."

Passing from one tier to the next, I spotted the names of movies I'd seen, and for an instant, a memorable scene would frame itself in my head... Paul Muni on the lam at the end of *I Am a Fugitive from a Chain Gang,* retreating from his woman and into the night as she asks him, "How will you live?" And Muni answering with a desperation that has always made me believe that he is still out there somewhere hiding out, "I steal!" Martha Vickers in *The Big Sleep* expressing to Humphrey Bogart on the occasion of their first meeting that she thought he was taller. And Bogart saying, "I tried to be." Gloria Swanson at the end of *Sunset Boulevard* confusing her arrest for murder with a press conference announcing her comeback into motion pictures, with the camera blurring her face as she says the film's last line, "I'm ready for my close-up!" Spencer Tracy as Stanley looking for Dr. Livingstone in *Stanley and Livingstone* coming to an East African village where it is rumored that a white man has been seen. Unfortunately, it isn't Dr. Livingstone but an albino. When Stanley's sidekick asks one of the tribesmen if the albino is a black-white man, the tribesman says, "No, he's a white-black man!"

"Here's the John Wayne section," Otis said when we reached the last level. "They got everything the Duke has done since 1939 when he made *Stagecoach*. That's when he really started to work his show with that yippy-yi-yay shit. Look, here's *They Were Expendable, The Fighting Seabees, Back to Bataan,* and *Sands of Iwo Jima.* That's the one that really fucked me around."

When Otis had all the prints he wanted, we went back upstairs to one of the projection rooms.

"You need any help?" I asked as he struggled to put a film on the projection reel with his left hand.

"No, it's more fun this way... You know, when I was in the Nam there was this village called Ben Sue that was rumored to be sympathetic to the VC. But army intelligence was never able to prove it. So they finally ordered the destruction of the village. Bulldozers came in and leveled Ben Sue to the ground. There wasn't even a trace that it ever existed. These flicks did to my mind what them bulldozers did to Ben Sue. The funny thing is, I can't stop watching them. There's something in me that still wants to believe that the Nam was like what we used to see in the movies... You remember *A Walk in the Sun?*"

"Yeah."

"I run this scene over and over because a this dude, the one pointing up at the plane and saying 'Look!' See how he got it in the mouth? Right in the middle of a word. That's the way it was in the Nam. The VC didn't wait around for you to finish a sentence before they interrupted your train of thought with a mortar...

"Lemme run this clip of *Sands of Iwo Jima*... Remember this part where they makin the invasion of the island... Oh shit! Blew that Jap pillbox up... Check this part right here... *Got* damn... Uh-oh, there they go with the flag... Ira Hayes is the last one in the back... Look—he never even got his hand on it..."

"Otis!"

"This is where John Wayne gets it... Check the Jap playin possum! You gotta give it to the Duke, though. He played the good part. He gets it right after he lights up that cigarette. Blew that sucker away! See that bullet hole burnin in his back right below where it says 'Sergeant Stryker.' Watch John Agar empty a whole clip in that Jap... He definitely gave him a Japanese rupture—One Ball Hung Lo!"

"Otis!"

"This is the part I like, when John Agar raps. I know it by heart. 'Aw right, you Marines, let's saddle up and get back in the war.' That reminds me of that scene in *The Longest Day*, about the Normandy invasion, when a whole company was pinned down on Omaha Beach and would not advance. Then Robert Mitchum comes up and says, 'There's only two kinds of men on this beach: those who are already dead and those who are about to die. So get up off your butts and move out!'"

"Otis, the film snapped!" I said, cutting on the lights. He cut off the projector, looked at the reams of film on the floor, and shot a defensive glance at me.

"What the fuck you lookin at?"

"What do you mean?"

"You think I've flipped out, don't you?"

"No, I don't think that."

"Yes, you do, muthafucka. I ain't stupid. Just cause you didn't go in the service you think you better than me."

"That's not true, Otis."

"You callin me a liar, muthafucka?" he said, rushing at me, slamming me into the wall and setting off the alarm. For the instant I was pressed against the wall, hate spit out at me from his eyes like darts. Then we stumbled and tripped our way out of the building, hunching into getaway profiles and hoisting our legs chin-high up Tenth Avenue until a police car pulled alongside of us.

"All right, you two, hold it right there," came the voice of one of the cops over a loudspeaker on the top of the patrol car. On the roof the red and white of a beacon chased each other in a circle as the two cops emerged from the car. They were huge hulks in blue uniforms, lumpy from overcrowded pockets. As they moved closer, their white faces showed the strain of fatigue. One stayed back a few feet while the other walked right up to us. Both had their hands within short reach of their guns.

"What's the hurry?" the closer one to us asked.

"Well, Officer, it's like this," Otis said, "me and my friend haven't seen each other in a long time, and we were reminiscing about the time when we used to run the mile relay in high school. My man here was third and I was anchor man. So when you saw us, we were reliving the hand-off-on-the-gun lap."

The cop turned around and looked at his partner, who shook

his head. Turning back to us, he said, "You expect us to go for that?"

"It's the truth," Otis said.

"It may be but it ain't good enough. You see, if you're a cop in the streets everybody's got a story for you. If you hear good ones, this ain't a bad job. So we bust people according to the stories they tell. If you can't tell a good story, you got to take a bust. Based on that first story, you two ain't doing too good. That's the way it is. It's our asses if we work a whole shift without making any busts and don't have any stories to show for the time. Most cops would rather have the stories. It makes our job easier and a lot more fun…

"But times have changed. People seem to have lost the knack for talking their way out of trouble. So we got to make more busts. It's a shame cause cops in every precinct in the city are starving for good stories… Now, I got a proposition for you two. We're almost at the end of our shift and we're tired. But we ain't made a bust all night. You two fit a lot of descriptions and we could take you in just on that. But we'd rather hear a story. A good one this time." Otis started to speak. "Unh, unh," the cop cut in, "I want to hear from you this time," he said, pointing to me.

"Well, it's like this," I said. "We were running out of respect for Mantan Moreland, who used to play the chauffeur, Birmingham Brown, in all those old Charlie Chan movies. We always dug Birmingham because he knew when the plot of a whodunit thickened he couldn't depend on his gig. So when push not only came to shove but was riding piggyback, Birmingham would say 'Feets, do your stuff.'

"His best movie was *From the Back of the Bus to the Driver's Seat,* which was set in the Deep South. Charlie Chan and Birmingham are on a bus trip in search of two dudes named Plessy and Ferguson, who are believed to be running an organization called 'Separate but Equal Unlimited,' which is really a front for an international syndicate that manufactures and distributes trick bags and sleight-of-hand gadgets...

"Plessy and Ferguson are believed to be on the bus, so in an attempt to find out who they are, Birmingham cops a squat in the front and goes into what he calls his 'indefinite routine,' where he talks to himself and then interrupts himself with some off-the-wall rap from a second party who is not present. This causes many whites to change their seats. In different parts of the bus are some of Birmingham's cut buddies from the Limousine and Rickshaw Union who are disguised in whiteface. Whenever somebody white sits next to them they badmouth Birmingham for his disgraceful behavior and express their agreement with the Booker T. Washington philosophy that, in all things social, blacks and whites should be as separate as the fingers on a hand. One man finally goes for the bait and tries to interest one of the dudes in whiteface in some stock in 'Separate but Equal Unlimited.'

"The bust is made and the man turns out to be Plessy. At first Plessy refuses to point out Ferguson, but changes his mind when Charlie Chan threatens him with separate but unequal punishment... As Charlie Chan's rickshaw man, Birmingham was able to expose the hype behind 'Separate but Equal Unlimited' because he knew that one could be in the driver's seat and still be taken for a ride... So, at least once a day we honor Birmingham Brown by invoking his creed—'Feets, do your stuff'—which is what we were doing when you stopped us."

The cop turned around to his partner again, who shrugged and shook his head up and down.

"All right. You two can go. You definitely got a lot of shit with you. But if we catch you again you better not run the same shit on us, cause if you do, we'll make both your faces break out into assholes!"

"Well," Otis said as we waited for a cab, "it looks like all that shit you learned in college finally paid off."

OTIS AND I DIDN'T SPEAK at all on the ride back uptown. When we got to Wells' it was dawn. I figured Alice would be pissed by my getting there over an hour past the time I said I would meet her. Wells' had a pretty good-size crowd made up of people who were probably still high from Friday night and had a bad case of the munchies. Alice and Pauline were in a booth in the rear of the restaurant.

"We had just about given you two up," Pauline said. Alice didn't say anything; Otis sat down and looked up at the ceiling.

"Sorry I'm late," I said to Alice.

"Sorry didn't do it," she said. I ordered and went up to the front, put some money in the jukebox, and played a side as a way of apologizing to Alice.

"You always let records do your talking?" Otis asked when I sat back down. "Hey, I'm talking to you, man." I continued to ignore him. "I bet you let dudes fuck you in the ass the whole time you was in the joint."

"Maybe if I'd gone in the service like you, I'd be more together," I said.

"That's the difference between you and me. I don't let nobody fuck with me!"

"When's the last time you looked at the end of your arm?"

"I'm still twice the man you'll ever be. And if you don't believe me, hit the floor, muthafucka!"

"No thanks, Otis. I'm through playing your games."

"Through? Shit, you ain't never played, chump. I carried your ass all those years. I thought there might be some more to you after you got out the joint. But you ain't never gonna be the real thing... What I need is somebody to keep me in shape. Like that dude sitting behind you."

He was sitting alone, sporting a black wide-brimmed hat, broken-down ace, deuce, trey, a ruby-red suit, and rings that looked like pieces of planets. There was a worm of a scar on the side of his face that jerked when he ate.

"He looks a lot like Slick Swanson. He probably thinks he's slick too. I think I'll go over and find out what he's into."

"You better be cool, Otis."

"No, you be cool, punk! You're good at it. And anyway, push ain't gonna come to shove unless I'm the one doin the shovin." He got up and walked over to the dude's table.

"Excuse me, home," Otis said, "but has anyone ever told you, you resemble Slick Swanson, the disc jockey?"

The dude looked up from his plate, pried some food loose from between his teeth with a fingernail, and sucked his teeth.

"Yeah, you just did."

"Well, I just wanted to know if you were aware of it."

"Is there anything else you wanna hip me to?"

"No, that's about it—except do you believe that style is character?"

"Okay, my man, I think you better raise."

"Hey, there's no need to get an attitude. I just wanted to ask you a few questions."

"Did you hear what I said?"

"Yeah, I heard you, but—" It was a slap, snapping Otis' head around to the limit and sending him crashing into a table. I looked at Otis: We had both aspired to the same fantasies about being bad, but the humiliation twitching in his face was the reason I never had the courage of mine. The other dude's face looked bone hard and leather tough from living in the saddle of do or die. He had sized up Otis and knew what he was capable of.

"You said style was character, didn't you, home? Well, let's see some."

"Please, let's not have any trouble," the waitress pleaded.

"Don't worry, Mama, there ain't gonna be no trouble. Ask him... How much do I owe you? You're very greasy, my man, but you got a long way to slide before you get to be as slick as me," he said on his way out.

"Forget it, Otis," I said, but he burned out of Wells' like a flame sucking quickly down a fuse to a stick of dynamite. I ran after him as he moved his arms in a way that resembled the language of mutes. His legs slid at angles as if he was doing the Twist in slow motion. The other man stood at the corner rearing back on his heels, coattail flung back, his right arm cocked on his hip.

Propelling himself toward the other man, sucking in air as he moved, Otis slammed into him and they stuck together. Then the dude stepped away and disappeared around the corner. Otis tottered and fell backward in a heap on the pavement. The flash of something metallic protruded from his stomach like a grave marker. I kneeled over him, watching his contorted face struggle to shape sounds that wouldn't come out. His body writhed around the knife stuck in his belly. I reached for it, but my hand became spastic as my eyes fastened on the blood spreading like shade through his shirt till it hugged him skintight.

I pushed a path through the gathering crowd of people.

"Hey, where you going, man?"

"He's not the one that did it."

"What happened?"

"Some dude shanked the cat."

"He split around the corner."

"Anybody call the police?"

"Yeah."

"Somebody ought to call an ambulance."

"He'll bleed to death before they get here."

"Crazy muthafucka got what his hand called for. Didn't have no business comin at that dude the way he did."

"Aw, man, the dude slapped him. What would you done?"

"I sure wouldn't have let the dude know what I was going to do!"

"Yeah, he should a snuck him."

Moving beyond the range of voices, I found myself in the midst of a group of kids.

"You should a seen it."

"Yeah, it was cool, man."

"What happened?"

"Somebody got stabbed trying to do some kung fu."

"Oh, yeah?"

"Yeah. The faggot-ass muthafucka didn't even know how to do it right. If that had a been me I would a kicked that muthafucka to death. He wouldn't a stabbed me!"

"Aw, punk. You wouldn't a done nothin but ran to your mama. You ain't nothin. You let a white boy whip your ass."

"Oh, yeah?" he said. Bringing his forearms in against his sides, he went into a squat, raised his bent right leg into a jackknife, and snapped his foot straight into the side of the other boy's head.

"Eeeeyowwww!" The boy ran screaming to the curb and from the debris picked up a drained wine bottle that he broke against a fire hydrant. The shatter of the bottle moved the heat of attention from Otis to the spectacle of the two boys. The boy who had done the kicking stood his ground while the other boy advanced on him with the broken bottle. Suddenly, involuntary muscles activating me thrust me between the two boys.

"Gimme that bottle!" I yelled, reaching for his arm. Fear and surprise detonated in his face. He swung at my hand. I snatched it back to see a stream of blood flooding between my fingers.

He jabbed at me again with the bottle. I jerked away too late. But before the pain spoke from the place where I was cut, I replayed in slow motion the broken bottle pushing into my side, the give and take, and finally feeling the raggedy mouth of the wine bottle cut into me. I ran, my head thrown back, my throat gargling the screams from the street and the sirens in the distance.

I RAN INTO A FIRE HYDRANT. Dizziness from my eyes formed a cartoon blurb above my head, filling up with diacritical marks and exclamation points.

"You ain't nuthin," someone said. There was a man leaning against a pole of a bus stop sign shaking his head. "You couldn't even take a bottle away from a kid. You ain't nuthin but a silly-assed little mama's boy."

A boy resembling me ran into a building. I followed him and knocked on a door to one of the rooms.

"Just a minute, Melvin, I'm dressing."

"Mama, how come I can't watch you when you dressing?"

"It's not polite for a little boy your age to watch his mother when she's not dressed."

"But you see me when I'm not dressed."

"That's different, Melvin. I'm your mother. I brought you into the world."

"Mama, when you brought me into the world was you dressed then?"

"No, Melvin, I wasn't."

"Mama, could you bring me into the world again so I could see you when you ain't dressed?"

"Come on in here, Melvin, and zipper me up!"

The room was engulfed by thick grass, twigs, and high weeds. A wind bent the weeds into bows, and in the opening between, was an elderly woman wearing coveralls, white tennis sneakers, and a Brooklyn Dodger baseball cap. It was Mrs. Cotton and she was looking intently at a small patch of earth cordoned off by pegs and string.

"Miz Cotton?"

"I see you all set, Melvin. Well, remember what I said and do something even if you only spit." The weeds snapped back into unstrung bows, swallowing up Mrs. Cotton.

I made an oval shape with my hands around my mouth and yelled through the opening.

"Whoooahhh. Whoooahhh. Whoooahhh." Within seconds, similar cries echoed from every direction. The weeds wobbled and fell flat to the earth. About eight other boys were visible. They were all decked out in a patchwork of clothes trying to get next to Western dress.

"Okay, let's go!" A cap pistol was fired.

"Hey, man, I got you in the arm."

"No, you didn't. You thought you got me. Like you thought like Nelly and thought shit was jelly."

"See that, man. I didn't sound on you."

"Aw, go suck a butt and hug a nut."

"Man, what's wrong with you? I told you to watch where you swinging."

"I didn't mean it. I slipped."

"Slip again, punk!"

"Don't be coughing in my face, Melvin. What's wrong with you?"

"I ran out of caps."

"You cough in my face again and I'm gonna run upside your head."

"But I got to cough and spit. I'm Doc Holliday."

"Damn, Melvin, you always got to mess up the game with some stupid shit."

"Yeah, drop your gun and cover your mouth." A chitlin-faced man was brought in on a stretcher and lifted into a highchair. He was wearing a judge's robe that collapsed around him. When he spoke he wheezed like an asthmatic.

"Will the defendant please step forward. Do you have anything to say on your behalf?"

"I only coughed because I was playing Doc Holliday."

"That's all well and good, Melvin, but the tradition of John Wayne requires that certain laws must be obeyed. Cowboys do not cough in each other's faces."

"But I ran out of caps!"

"That doesn't matter. The law is the law. If you are a cowboy and you get into trouble, you use a gun. You don't cough. Let me show you what I mean."

He reached into his robe and took out a spool of thread. He

removed a needle from the spool and broke off a long piece of thread. He licked one end of the thread and tried to see it through the eye of the needle. The effort proved too much for him and he fell back in his highchair exhausted.

"Se-eee what I mean? The laws of nature have rendered their verdict on my body, and I must have the serenity to accept them."

"But what's coughing got to do with that?"

"Coughing your way out of trouble is going against the laws of cowboys. And they must be accepted just like the laws of nature.

"Your behavior makes it clear to the court that you are in need of corrective detention. Your coughing and spitting are clear signs of your inability to make the appropriate responses during the rites of manhood."

"But it was the appropriate response for Doc Holliday."

"I'm sorry but I have no alternative but to sentence you to three years of hard labor at the state camp for fucking and fighting. During your term of incarceration you will be trained in the fine art of close-order knuckle drill, since the court believes that before you can fuck, you have to be able to fight. Parole will depend on your progress in performing satisfactorily in each of these two categories. The court usually grants the defendant the right to speak after sentencing, but your conduct thus far leads the court to suspect that something other than words will come from your mouth. Take him away!"

I was led to a door which had printed on it: WOLF TICKETS

AND ASS KICKING. The room was packed with men of the hard-headed and backbutted variety. Two dudes were in the center of the room louding each other. One of them was Otis.

"So what's your problem, man?

"I ain't got no problem. You got the problem."

"What's my problem?"

"Me, if you keep fucking with me!"

"Punk, you ain't gonna do nuthin but leave me alone."

"You believe that shit if you want to, but if I put hands on you, I'm takin your life!"

"Okay," Otis said, "this is an example of the proper way to sell a wolf ticket. Now, I'd like two more volunteers to try it." Chilly stepped forward. "Is there anyone else? What about you?"

"I just got here," I said.

"Well, there's no time like the present. Remember, he who hesitates is dead." The circle of men tightened around us, and Chilly bumped my shoulder.

"Hey, man, why don't you watch where you goin?" he said.

"I was watching where I was going," I said. "It's just that when such a frail-ass muthafucka like you walks down the street sideways I just automatically mark him absent."

"Awwww, SHIT!"

"Talk about him!"

As I turned my head to acknowledge the acclamation, something plunged into my chest and sucked back. In Chilly's hand was a pulsating mass of dripping tissue.

"I told you, you ain't nuthin. I snatched your heart out. And it don't even pump blood. It pumps Kool-Aid!"

"The chump don't have no heart!"

"Fuck him up!"

"Waste his ass!"

Guards whisked me out of there to another room. Behind a desk was a dude cut from a Sonny Liston mold.

"You have a problem, Ellington?"

"What's that?"

"You're off to a bad start in becoming a bronze buckaroo."

"I thought I sold a pretty good wolf ticket."

"Yeah, but all that's nullified when you let someone take your heart away from you. The value of a wolf ticket is having the heart to back it up. The baddest dudes usually don't have to do any more than sell the ticket."

"So what do I do now?"

"Well, the first thing is to get your heart back."

"How do I do that?"

"We put you in an arena with other dudes in your position. Then we turn out the lights and y'all commence to throwing hands."

"But what does that prove?"

"It proves that in the dark the ones who kick ass are those who bring the most ass."

"What happens if I don't bring enough ass?"

"That doesn't matter. It's a poor ass that can't take an ass-whipping anyway. So you can still get your heart back if you can do like a Timex watch and take a licking but keep on ticking. Now get out a here and let the doorknob hit where the good Lord split you!"

I waited in a den before being sent out to do battle with the rest of the heartless dudes.

A voice came over a loudspeaker.

"All right, everybody, it's time to bring ass. Just remember: the sweet smell of success comes from exposing somebody else's stink. Nobody will ever kiss your ass unless you kick theirs first. So let's see some decayed rump when the lights come up. Remember to keep in mind that all we're trying to do is prepare you for a world where nobody accidentally bumps into anyone else." The hatch to the den opened. There were hundreds of us in the arena.

"YOU GOT TO BRING ASS TO GET ASS!"

And then total darkness, followed by crazed shrieks, a stampede of hoofbeats, the crunch of bodies colliding, and blows backed up by grunts. I got caught in the height of someone's hitting streak, and fists spit into me without letup. Somehow I managed to drag myself to a neutral zone. A light shone on me and moved to my behind.

"Is his ass grass?"

"Yeah."

"Is it Kentucky Blue?"

"No, it looks more like crab to me."

"All right. Bring him along."

"Hey, looka here. It's the spade whose heart pumps Kool-Aid. What you got to say for yourself?"

"Well, the Chinese say that of the thirty-six ways of avoiding trouble, running is the best."

"Yeah, it figures that you'd be the first one to escape the scene of the action. And since you were the first to get away, we're going to parole you. But it will go down on your record that you were released because of your skill in evasive action."

I was picked up, and after a few warm-up tosses, thrown into a pool full of people being baptized. I was dunked until those giving the sacrament figured I was ready to enter my new church home. I was given a standing ovation. An apple-butter-brown man in ministerial robes with hair laid to his scalp like patent leather motioned me to the front of the church. My folks, Debra, Alice, Pauline, Otis, and Chilly were among the many packing the pews.

"At this time, we'd like to welcome our illustrious brother back among us and present him with a token of our appreciation for what he has done."

"What are you talking about?"

"We know you are modest, Melvin, but we heard the splendid reports of your work while you were away. And these have led us to the conclusion that in the future the sawdust from your good works will become a lasting residue in the nation's eyes, ears, nose, and throat. So, in recognition of the work you've done thus far, and as a testament to our confidence that you will continue the work you have begun, I would like, on behalf of everyone here, to present you with this hammer!"

The applause was deafening.

"Say something appropriate," the preacher whispered.

"I hope you don't mind if I don't make a long speech, but at this very moment I have an appointment to see a man about some lumber that will help to realize the work for which you are honoring me today. Thank you!"

Nodding to the congregation and the minister, I slipped out a side door that led to a courtyard bordered by tenements sagging from the weight of clothes hanging from clotheslines. In an alley leading away from the courtyard a man was sitting on a milk crate playing a guitar.

"I'm a MAN! / M, man, / A, a child, / N, non-spoiled! / I'm a MAANNN!" When he saw me, he stopped playing.

"Excuse me, I want to ask you about that song you were singing."

"I can't tell you nuthin bout it."

"But maybe if you could—"

"I can't do nuthin with your maybes, ifs, and supposes. You got to pay your own fare when you in the tragic magic." He got up and walked toward the back entrance of one of the buildings.

"Wait a minute!" I said, running after him. But he disappeared into the building. I tried to find an alley that led to the street. Then, from a space between one of the buildings, a boy came through carrying an open switchblade. There was a sharp pain in my left side. I touched it and my shirt was saturated with blood. I took my hand away and it began to throb with pain. I looked at it and there was a deep gash in my palm caked with blood. The boy moved on me. I turned to run but tripped. And he was on top of me with the switchblade poised over my face.

"You couldn't even take a bottle away from a kid." My focus on the blade shifted to where the voice came from. It was Chilly. "You know what I'm going to do for you, punk? I'm gonna let you see what your face looks like. Okay, peel off his face!"

I screamed in time to feel the sharp steel tug against the side of my jaw, but never saw the blade do its work as blood ran into my eyes.

"You got the face?"

"Yeah, I got it."

"All right. Give it to me."

"What do you mean, give it to you?"

"Just what I said."

"Unh, unh. It's mine."

"No, it's not. It's his. Now, either you give it to me or I'll take yours!"

"Shit!"

"Melvin?"

"Yeah."

"This is Hardknocks. Everything is cool, but whatever you do, don't open your eyes till I tell you."

"What happened to my face?"

"It'll be all right. But Chilly had that kid peel it to the bone. If he could have, he would've recast your mug in a mold to suit himself."

"Where's Chilly now?"

"He split... Now, dig this. I got your face heating up in a frying pan. But before I pour it back over your skull, I'm gonna hip you to a few ways of looking at yourself. Now, imagine that your mug is an egg, and think about all the different ways of fixing it. For example, soft-boiled is always hip-hugging for any mug, especially if you want to be together in a jiffy. Only thing is, you can't let folks get too close cause the slightest bump will crack your shell and show you as the raw recruit you are.

"Then there's hard-boiled. Now, that's a good shingle for the mug. Folks could peel you back from now on and never get to you. But then your bark would be so tough there might not be nuthin left of you. You could decide to leave your sunny side up and keep out of sight for a while with your once over light. And then, of course, there's the meanest mug breakout of all—scrambled. When you're scrambled, you can use a spatula and try to take the best from all the ways of fixing your face and risk being a little bit of everything.

"So what's it gonna be, Melvin? Sometimes you can't save the face and spare the ass at the same time. But whatever your face is gonna be, you decide. That way there's no squawk at bust-a-yolk time. Uh-oh, your mug's giving me uppity signs. Let me put it back. Don't move now. Just lie still."

I moaned as the hot flesh and blood splashed back into the hollow recesses of my skull. I felt my face cook to the bone tissue and stick into place. And as the juices of flesh and bone cooled, they turned to sweat, streaming over my face. I was delirious within the wet heat of my sweat when a lyric from a woman's voice broke my fever.

> Oh, they say some people long ago
> were searching for a different tune,
> one that they could croon
> as only they can.
> They only had the rhythm so
> they started swaying to and fro.
> They didn't know just what to use
> so that is how the bluuuues
> really
> really
> really, began...

I OPENED MY EYES to blurred images. I blinked repeatedly, and as my vision sharpened I could make out a large chalk-covered figure hovering over me. Searching the whiteness, I found a bush of hair the color of ash, a bean-pie-complexioned face punctured by sleepy liquid eyes with thick lids, cheeks, a chin, and a mouth grizzly with black hair flecked with gray.

"Where am I?"

"You're in the emergency ward of Harlem Hospital. You've been in shock from loss of blood. You were delirious when you were brought in here, and I had to give you a shot to calm you down. Your wounds have been dressed. You'll be all right. Just don't try to move around too much."

"How long have I been here?" I raised myself up on the bed and winced as I felt some pain within the tightness of the bandages on my left side. My right palm also throbbed with pain and I noticed that it, too, was heavily bandaged.

"You've been here over an hour."

"Who are you?"

"'I'm Doctor Blue."

"Where's Otis? What happened to him? Is he all right?"

"Your friend didn't make it."

I tried to summon something up from inside of me but nothing came. "Did they catch the dude who did it?"

"I don't think so. The police want to question you about the man who stabbed your friend and also about what happened to you. The people that were with you are also here, and your family has been contacted. But I told the police I'd let them know when you could talk to them. I don't want you to have too much excitement all at once. I think you've had enough for one night."

"Thanks."

"Well, my reasons are not entirely medical."

"Oh, no?"

"I wanted to talk to you. You interest me."

"Why is that?"

"Do you have any idea how many stabbings and gunshot wounds I treat every weekend?"

I shook my head.

"They're too many to count. But no matter how many dudes come through here, the reasons are always the same: money, pride, or a woman. To keep my sanity, I play a little game where I look at the wounds of every dude I treat and try to guess what category he falls under. I've gotten pretty good at it. Your friend was no problem. I guessed him right away. A simple case of trying to hide fear behind foolish pride. But you're a little more difficult. I haven't yet figured out what your problem is. Did you really try to take a bottle away from a kid?"

"Yeah, I tried."

"Why?"

"I don't know. I couldn't stop Otis from getting himself killed. I guess I figured I could stop those kids."

"Just because they were kids?"

"Yeah, I guess so."

"You guess! Don't you know?"

"Hey, look, Doctor Blue. I really don't feel like being psychoanalyzed, okay?"

"I'm sorry. I didn't mean to get on your case. I get a little carried away with my game sometimes. You can split if you want to."

I slid down off the bed slowly. On the counter next to the coatrack was a turntable with a stack of records on it.

"You play music in here?"

"You better believe it! Those sides keep me from becoming completely numb. Look, Ellington, I don't want to get in your business, but did you just get out of jail yesterday?"

"Yeah. Who told you?"

"One of the women you were with, named Alice."

"I guess you know what I was doing time for, too."

"Yeah, she told me about that. But what I can't understand is why you didn't cool out at home your first day out. Couldn't wait to get some pussy, eh? Yeah, I can dig it."

"Oh, you can, hunh? Well, tell me about it!"

"Oh, excuse me. I forgot. You're one of those cats who are willing to go to jail for a principle. And you'd never allow something as counterrevolutionary as pussy to even enter your mind... But tell me, Melvin, why didn't you go into the service?"

"I didn't feel I had anything to fight for."

"Look, don't tell me what you read in a book. Tell me your *own* reasons for not going in."

"I guess I just didn't understand how the army had a right to decide when I should put my life on the line."

"Do you always refuse to do something you don't understand?"

"It depends on what it is. And when it comes to my life, I figure I should have the final say on what I will or won't do."

"Well, tell me this, then. Did you think you were putting your life on the line when you grabbed that kid with the bottle?"

"I didn't really think about it."

"Your friend Otis didn't think about what he was doing either. And now he's dead."

"What are you trying to say?"

"Only that neither of you did very much thinking last night. The difference is that you came out alive. But only because you were dealing with kids."

"Yeah, but it was my choice."

"Then it was a bullshit choice."

"Hey, you don't know anything about me!"

"Maybe not, but I bet I'm close."

I leaned back against the bed to steady myself.

"Sit down on the bed for a minute," he said.

"Leave me alone!" I said, knocking his arm away. "You must really dig taking people apart."

"Hey, why not? I don't get any satisfaction trying to put them back together. Every weekend people come through here wasted. And for shit that don't even matter. And that's the funny part. When you get right down to it, none of it really matters. Hey, I want you to listen to something."

He went through a stack of records, found the one he was looking for, and put it on the turntable.

"I play this for people I treat who I figure can profit from it. It's a Miles Davis tune called *So What*. And that's the advice I give: that ultimately you should be able to say 'so what' to just about anything. That things really don't matter... Listen to this."

The opening statement of the theme by a full orchestra speaks of bad news, and the bass whispers, "Did you hear that?" The reeds and the wind instruments, backed up by the piano, loud the bass like it ain't no big thing. "So what." The bass is put out by the way everybody ganged up on him but takes it out on the keyboard, saying, "Hey, man, I just thought I'd pull your coat, but since you wanna get the ass I'm gonna sic Miles on you." And Miles comes on out the side of his mouth with licks that say, "Let me tell you about yourself, sucker." Miles' tricky-lipping slurs pose as threats, but the piano is insistent on the comeback chord: "I don't want to hear it. 'So what.'" Miles shapes his rap into spitting fancy lipwork, but the piano player is right back on time with an answer: "You don't understand..." "So what!" "Did you hear about..." "So what!" Miles feints and styles, then blows: "Well, later for you too, then, chump." And you hear the brass knuckles rattling in his tone as the tenor man is all up in the face of the refrain, "So what!" His solo is a wolf ticket signifying behind the dozens, with a little of my father talking mean through teeth and biting down on his lower lip. The tenor man takes his solo out, murder-mouthing the "so what" piano chord. The bass line reenters the rap, giving a synopsis of the theme with fat plucks on the string. But the piano man ain't impressed, saying, in so many words, "Yeah, I hear you, but ain't nobody put their hands on me." So the answer is still "So What," with the ax men going along with the piano man's chord... So what... So what... So what...

"You understand what I'm trying to say?"

"Yeah, I guess so. But that's like saying nothing matters."

"Nothing does."

"Some things matter."

"What are they?"

"What you do here matters."

"No it doesn't."

"Then why do you stay?"

"Because this is what I do best."

"Then it matters."

"No it doesn't. My being here or not being here doesn't change a thing. What I do could be good, bad, or indifferent. It still doesn't make any difference."

"But if it's important to you, then that makes the difference."

"Bullshit!"

"You're wrong."

"Shit. Do you think you changed anything by what you did? You'd a done better letting them kids kill each other. That kid that cut you probably feels he can get away with anything now."

"But I didn't do what I did for those kids. I did it for myself. And you know, that was the first time I can remember doing something where I wasn't trying to prove something to some-body else?"

"And you damn near got yourself killed for your trouble."

"Well, at least it was my doing and not anyone else's."

"You're a fool."

"So what!"

"Touché!"

"I think I'm feeling well enough to leave now," I said.

"All right. You can go."

"Take it easy, Doctor Blue."

"No, I doubt if I'll take it at all."

I looked through a glass and saw Alice, Pauline, my mother and father, and my sister Debra. A version of the opening statement of the theme to "So What" played in my head. Why wasn't there a dirge in my slide for Otis? Would Alice help me help us both out of the wee hours of the blues? Would Pauline jump on my case with her usual "Now, ain't this some shit?" line? Would Debra and my folks send me through all kinds of changes? Was Doctor Blue right about me being a fool? I walked out into all of that and all the rest, hoping I'd be able to play the chord changes between what I did mind and what didn't matter.

ONE LAST RIFF BEFORE
WE HIT IT AND QUIT...

IT WAS WITH A STRANGE ELATION that a week later I found myself alone with Alice. She had invited me over for dinner, and after we'd eaten, I felt guilty that my thoughts were on going to bed with her and not on Otis' funeral, which had been earlier in the day.

"It's still hard for me to believe that Otis is dead," I said.

"Hard or easy, it's all the same," she said.

"I guess you're right. You know, I still haven't been able to feel anything behind his death."

"What do you want to feel?" she asked.

"Something."

"Oh, come on, Melvin! Otis was never your friend."

"Maybe that's what's been bothering me—knowing that I hated him all those years we were supposed to be so tight. And now that he's dead, feeling guilty about it."

"That's nothing to feel guilty about. I can see why you resented him. I never understood why you let him make you his flunky. If I were you, I wouldn't lose any sleep over it. But, Melvin, you've always been hung up on what you're supposed to feel, and not what you do feel. You want to be on everybody's side but your own."

We were on the couch and she was sitting with her legs crossed with the right foot tucked behind the left ankle. I followed the way her finely whittled body weaved its way vinelike up into the couch.

"How're you doing?" she asked.

"I'm all right. Still a little sore, that's all."

"Does that hurt?" she asked, sliding her hand along the left side of my rib cage.

"Unh, unh," I lied. She continued rubbing, moving her hand in a slow, waxing motion up into my chest. Our breathing became labored and loud enough to be heard. I cupped her face tentatively in my hands as if to make sure she was real.

"It's been a long time," I said.

"For me, too," she said.

"I'm not sure I'm gonna know how to act."

"I think you'll remember," she said.

Our mouths met and I sucked back the pungent taste of brandy, nicotine, and onions. She moved her mouth to my ear and drove me to moaning with the flicking of her quick tongue. "Let's go in the bedroom," she whispered with my ear still in her mouth.

I had no sense of undressing as my rising desire for Alice seemed to pressure the clothes right off me. As she undressed, the light from a shaded floor lamp caught the cognac color of her body. We got into bed and I lay my hands on her feverishly, wanting to do everything at once. My mouth found its hunger in her sweet and sour mouth, under her arms, on her breasts, in the creases of her navel, at the peak of her thighs, behind her knees, and on her fingers and toes. Her taste was sweet soap mixed with the salty moisture of her heated odor.

Rolling around the bed like tumbleweed, we finally came to a stop with Alice on top of me. She reached between my legs and as I swelled she sucked and cowlicked me into a frenzy. Moving over top of me, she lowered herself down, guiding me until I was inside her. The feel of how snug we fit set my whole body on fire. We began to move and when my stomach hollowed out in a contraction, her rounded pelvis drove into the space, pushing me deeper inside her. The sheets of the bed hissed under us as our stomachs made a click song, and sweat washed up against the shore of our ribs.

My mouth locked open, but I couldn't catch enough breath to scream. Tears stung my eyes.

"Ohhh shit! God damn, baby! What you trying to do, make butter?"

"Yeah, that's right! Yeah! Yeah! Yeah!" she panted without missing a stroke in the insistent churn of her hips. I was in a crazed state, bucking to come and at the same time not wanting to spend myself. I pounded my fists into the bed; then kneaded Alice's back with my hands and finally let them ride her writhing behind. But if you move you lose! If you Move you Lose! If You Move You Lose! IF YOU MOVE YOU LOSE!

Lying in the wetness and smell of spent desire, we were curled back to front into spoons with me contracted into Alice's back.

"Melvin?"

"Yeah."

"You remember what I said at that party when you asked me if I liked to fight?"

"I remember."

"Well, I'm serious about that. If I can't fight with whoever I'm with, I'd rather be alone."

"But what do you mean by fight?"

"I'm not talking about being beat up on, but living my life in a certain way. For a long time I didn't care enough about myself to fight for the way I wanted to live. So I let myself get fucked over by men I didn't even care about. It's taken me a while to come out of that, but now I'm at the point where I'm not going to use myself up anymore with men I don't care enough about to fight with. I like you, Melvin, but we won't get along if you don't fight or try to stop me from fighting."

We didn't say any more. There was only the hush of our bodies laboring slowly, slightly apart. Everything that had happened over the last week had taken a lot out of me, and listening to Alice gave me the jitters. She was definitely up to something more than a little light sport. But I figured I had done enough fighting for a while and didn't know if I had the energy to get conjugated with her. A part of me wanted to renege on everything and just lay dead. Hadn't I earned that right? I had paid my dues. Yet what I would trade off by basking in the non-use of myself could be even worse, since a thing never meant a thing until it moved.

I pulled Alice's full spoon-shape closer to me.

ACKNOWLEDGMENTS

I would like to express my gratitude to Erica Vital-Lazare for her enthusiastic championing of *Tragic Magic* as part of the inauguration of McSweeney's OF THE DIASPORA; to Amanda Uhle for her unstinting efforts, shepherding the novel to publication; to Frank Johnson for all he's done to introduce *Tragic Magic* to a new generation of readers; and to Ismail Muhammad for his generous foreword, which enlightened me with its engagingly fresh perspective.

ABOUT THE AUTHOR

WESLEY BROWN is an acclaimed novelist, playwright, and teacher. He worked with the Mississippi Freedom Democratic Party in 1965 and became a member of the Black Panther Party in 1968. In 1972, he was sentenced to three years in prison for refusing induction into the armed services and spent 18 months in Lewisburg Federal Penitentiary. For 26 years, Brown was a much-revered professor at Rutgers University, where he inspired hundreds of students. He currently teaches literature at Bard College at Simon's Rock and lives in Chatham, New York.

OF THE DIASPORA

A BOOK SERIES FROM McSWEENEY'S

OF THE DIASPORA is a series of previously published works in Black literature whose themes, settings, characterizations, and conflicts evoke an experience, language, imagery, and power born of the Middle Passage and the particular aesthetic which connects African-derived peoples to a shared artistic and ancestral past. The first novel in the series is *Tragic Magic* by Wesley Brown, originally published in 1978 and championed by Toni Morrison during her tenure as an editor at Random House. It's followed by *Praisesong for the Widow,* a novel by Paule Marshall originally published in 1983 and a recipient of the Before Columbus Foundation American Book Award. The third book is a collection of editorial photography by Lester Sloan framed within a conversation with his daughter, Aisha Sabatini Sloan.

The series is edited by Erica Vital-Lazare, a professor of creative writing and marginalized voices in literature at the College of Southern Nevada. Published in collectible hardcover editions with original cover art by Sunra Thompson, the first three works hail from Black American voices defined by what Amiri Baraka described as a strong feeling "getting into new blues, from the old ones." OF THE DIASPORA—North America will be followed by series from the diasporic communities of Europe, the Caribbean, and Brazil.

Other books in the OF THE DIASPORA *series:*

PRAISESONG FOR THE WIDOW
by Paule Marshall

Avey Johnson—a Black, middle-aged, middle-class widow—has long since put behind her the Harlem of her childhood. Suddenly, on a cruise to the Caribbean, she packs her bag in the middle of the night and abandons her friends at the next port of call. The unexpected and beautiful adventure that follows provides Avey with the links to the culture and history she has so long disavowed. Originally published in 1983, and a recipient of the Before Columbus Foundation American Book Award.

CAPTIONING THE ARCHIVES:
A CONVERSATION IN
PHOTOGRAPHS AND TEXT
Photos by Lester Sloan; text by Aisha Sabatini Sloan

In this father-daughter collaboration, photographer Lester Sloan opened his archive of street photography, portraits, and news photos, and noted essayist Aisha Sabatini Sloan interviewed him, creating rich, probing, dialogue-based captions for more than one hundred photographs.

Available at bookstores, and at store.mcsweeneys.net